PRAISE FOR M. B. GOFFSTEIN

"Goffstein is a minimalist, but her text and pictures carry the same emotional freight as William Blake's admonishment to see the world in a grain of sand and eternity in an hour."

—*Time* magazine

"M. B. Goffstein is one of the finest illustrator/writers of our time. Like porcelain, there is more to her work than meets the eye. Beneath the delicacy and fragility is a core of astounding strength."

—*Washington Post*

"A book by M. B. Goffstein is a beautifully simple and simply beautiful thing."

—*New York Times Book Review*

"One of the few modern author-illustrators who are assured classic status."

—*Publishers Weekly*

"It's good to have a Goffstein! She unearths the treasure of simplicity."

—*New York Times Book Review*

THE COLLECTED WRITINGS OF M. B. GOFFSTEIN

Words Alone: Twenty-Six Books Without Pictures

Art Girls Together: Two Novels

Daisy Summerfield's Art: The Complete Flea Market Mysteries

Biography of Miss Go Chi: Novelettos & Poems

DAISY
SUMMERFIELD'S
ART

M. B. Goffstein

DAISY SUMMERFIELD'S
ART

The Complete Flea Market Mysteries

DAVID ALLENDER PUBLISHER

DAVID ALLENDER PUBLISHER
is devoted to the work of author-artist
M. B. Goffstein (1940–2017).

··

David Allender Publisher, New York

Back cover photograph by Kohno Toshihiko

ISBN: 978-1-949310-03-0
e-ISBN: 978-1-949310-05-4

FIRST EDITION

A painting requires a little mystery...

—EDGAR DEGAS

CONTENTS

DAISY
SUMMERFIELD'S
ART

A Little Cracked

1989

THURSDAY

Women in their late forties are beautiful. Daisy Summerfield's beauty came from carving wood and stone.

She sat in the office of the president of the Kodaly Gallery feeling very happy and at home. How long had it been? It was stupid to avoid her friends.

Alan Kodaly, straight and slim, dark hair graying, dark eyes shining, crooked teeth showing in his smile, was saying, "It's the top museum in this country! I think you should do it."

Daisy was having such a nice time, she hated to wreck it by disappointing Alan. She had never taken an assignment and couldn't start now.

She was sorry. Since Daisy had stopped sculpting, she'd lost daily contact with the Kodaly Gallery. Sometimes she was so lonely she wished for a mouse in her studio apartment.

"—it has been, what, four years?" Alan looked at her kindly.

Daisy picked up the photo on Alan's desk.

"He's cute," she managed. "You know, I really would like to do a portrait. I read *A Giacometti Portrait* so many times! Why did he choose me?"

"He likes your work."

"I've been thinking about working in porcelain clay, solid shapes with words cut in them."

"What kind of words?"

"A flat block scalloped on top would say 'Pickle Dish.'"

"Hmm."

"It could be a whole series called Every Day China."

"Hnh?"

"But so far the pickle dish is the only shape that interests me."

"Huh."

What was she saying? Was the flea market making her lose her mind?

"Here," Alan said. "Take his photo and let me know what you decide."

Had it really been four years since Daisy had brought him new work? She was embarrassed, and that reminded her why she had stayed away.

Alan brought their meeting to a close and he helped her on with her coat.

It was a cold January day in New York City and tomorrow, people said, would be even colder. At the end of the street, to the west across Fifth Avenue, was the Metropolitan Museum. The temperature didn't keep large groups from venturing out in pursuit of culture or whatever it was they hoped to find.

Daisy walked in the opposite direction, east to Madison Avenue and James Rose Antique China.

From the china shop came a short man wearing a fur coat.

"You must be insane," she said as she flung the door away from him and went in.

He was John Lorimer. She had his picture in her pocket.

Behind an elaborate desk, the Roses were at the rear of the shop. Slowly, Daisy moved to the back to hear what they were saying.

"I'm sorry. We're closed. We have an emergency," Mrs. Rose said, walking her to the door.

Daisy stepped over the sill and heard the lock click behind her.

She stood outside pretending to look at a modern pot in the uptown window. She saw James Rose speak angrily to his son, Leon.

To Daisy's side, two men came to the door.

"They're closed," she said, as the buzzer sounded and they went in.

Superimposed on the glass between her and the rose-bordered cups was a blue-and-white police car.

"DAISY!"

Daphne Kodaly looked down Madison, made a judgment, and ran across.

"Alan said you just left."

"I wanted to look at china."

"They were robbed!"

"ARE THOSE rose-cut diamonds?" Daisy asked, as they took off their coats at the Camilla Coffee Shop.

"Yes, do you like them? Just coffee for me, Oscar."

Daisy ordered a toasted bagel.

Daphne looked great, as always; her auburn hair had been freshly colored and arranged in a French twist.

Daisy's faded blond ponytail was clasped in a blue-and-pink plastic barrette.

"Alan and I are going to a dinner at the museum tonight. We'll make them set a place for you, if you want to choose a husband."

"Not until I'm sixty."

"You could meet John Lorimer. I think the portrait is a wonderful idea."

"I just saw him leave James Rose wearing a fur coat!"

"Here we go," thought Daphne.

"Are you working?" Daphne asked. "Maybe you need this commission as motivation."

Daisy didn't work if she didn't have a problem to solve, and the exciting thing is that one problem could create fifty solutions. That was how she had carved the large body of work called Witnesses.

"I was just telling Alan that I've been thinking about working in clay."

"You made those figures, years ago."

They smiled at each other.

But the idea, a combination of Brancusi and antique china, was already dying. An artist can have ideas, she believed, but unless they are impossible, they won't be art.

"THE WORK itself—what is it? Something for museums or rich people to own," she'd told a class at Parsons earlier that week. "If you saw it lying on the street, would you recognize it?"

A young woman got very angry and red in the face. "I think art is, you know, *art*. Inspirational."

"It is altogether fitting and proper that you should," Daisy said. "But in a larger sense, we can not dedicate, we can not consecrate, we cannot hallow this ground. The brave men and women, living and dead, who struggled here have consecrated it far above our poor power to add or detract.

"The world will little note, nor long remember what we say here, but it can never forget what they did here. It is for us the living, rather, to be dedicated here to the unfinished work which they who fought here have thus far so nobly advanced."

The students glanced at each other, maybe not recognizing the Gettysburg Address.

Deathly tired, Daisy walked to the subway just when the high schools let out, and rode uptown in a car filled with nervous teenagers.

At Fiftieth Street they got out and had a gunfight on the platform.

An old woman rolled right under the bench Daisy was sitting on.

Everyone else hit the floor.

Daisy, last and least dramatic, knelt.

Then they had to avoid stepping on shell casings and get uptown some other way.

FRIDAY

"Go out and get the paper," Daphne said excitedly on the phone. "I can't talk. I'll be late for my seminar."

Daphne taught art history at The Fallone Institute. She had done her doctorate on her great love, the nineteenth-century artist George Bellows.

Gingerly carrying the *Times* and the *Post*, Daisy crossed Broadway and walked up to the Argo Diner.

BUTTERFINGERS! said a headline. "Rare Cup Found and Lost."

Daisy spread jam on her pancakes while she read.

TEMPEST IN A TEACUP

A teacup vanished from James Rose Antique China on Madison Avenue at 1:30 p.m. on Monday.

"I just turned around and it was gone," stated James Rose, 74.

"When we think of what this discovery would mean to ceramic scholars, we are devastated by its loss."

The blue cup discovered by James Rose, who declined to say where or how he found it, may be the only one of its kind.

"They found it at the flea market," thought Daisy.

Made by the Elers brothers, Dutch emigrant potters who worked in North Staffordshire, England, from 1690 to 1700, only a few of their teapots are known to exist and no teacups—until now.

SHE CALLED Daphne that night.

"Any more news?"

"Not about the robbery, but you know Leon Rose, James' son? He quit and walked out."

"No!" Daisy exclaimed. "He was my favorite Rose!"

"Mine, too. Oh, I forgot to ask!" Daphne said. "Will you help me choose bases for two Lachaise bronzes?"

"I'd love to!"

They agreed to meet at the Sculpture Shop a week from Sunday.

DAISY OPENED her china cabinet and took out her I-Hsing teapot.

The unglazed red stoneware shaped like a gourd had a narrow, curving spout and loop handle.

These were the teapots, sent to England with tea from China, that the Elers brothers were copying.

SATURDAY

If you're moving to New York, don't forget to pack a sweater.

Daisy lived in a good building on the Upper West Side at Eighty-Sixth Street and Broadway. There were regular oil deliveries and the boiler rarely broke.

Heat came up through some of the walls, but sometimes it got so cold she had to turn on a radiator. That made it so hot she had to open a window—not an easy task—and by the time she managed to turn off the radiator, it was freezing.

The windows of Daisy's studio apartment looked out on a well on the east side of her building. From her kitchen and bathroom windows she could see the street.

She didn't have a view but she got diffuse light, and every morning she heard crows caw and seagulls cry.

It was freezing outside. "I'd be crazy to go," she thought, leaving her building's warm vestibule.

The downtown IRT subway was on the west side of Broadway. She waited for the light, crossed the two thoroughfares, and went down the subway steps.

At Thirty-Fourth Street she put away her book. At Twenty-Eighth she got out.

The dark green globe above the railing looked like a head. It scared her every time.

There were few pedestrians on the street on a winter weekend morning. As she approached Sixth Avenue, she saw the vans in the parking lot.

THERE WERE only a few dealers braving the low temperatures, and they were scattered all around.

"Where's your hat?" asked Mr. Flea.

"I didn't know it was this cold." She shivered.

"It's *cold*."

She sometimes bought small things from him. She asked to see a sparkly ring in his glass case.

Some of the silver paint had peeled away, leaving gray plastic underneath.

"Oh, oh, oh," he cried. "Did you see the way that sparkled? That scares me. When something sparkles like that, I get *scared*!"

The magic of his little boy's hopefulness might make it a real diamond for the right customer.

Daisy tried it on, but it didn't fit.

"THAT'S A dollar," a man called past his wife from the cab of his dirty old truck.

Daisy put down the saucer.

"Anything you see on that table's a dollar," he called to her.

She wanted to cry "Let me in your truck" but thanked him and walked away.

Daisy looked through a box of white plastic charms and tried to hand it back to a dealer who was describing the layers she was wearing for warmth.

Forced to stand and listen to her, Daisy saw that some of her teeth were missing. Many dealers had missing teeth. Daisy admired their freedom from middle-class values.

She made her way to the last table before the gate. The booth was directly across from the manager's hut, used by the man she always saw carrying a clipboard.

Rummaging through a carton under the table, Daisy found a little bundle of burlap. Inside was a small blue cup.

In spots where the dull blue paint was missing, the cup was creamy white. A bouquet of flowers was sprigged onto it. The entire cup might have been molded, but she couldn't find any evidence of seams.

Someone had sprayed paint on the convex base. A tiny impressed x or y was filled with gold paint.

She was sure the blue and gold colors were added by someone who wanted to make the cup prettier. It could come off with the right solvent, she thought.

Daisy found the dealer behind a TV tray, nearly hidden under a tent rigged with a tarp. He wore a hood pulled tight around his face and was wrapped in a large flowered quilt.

She said, "You must be frozen! Can I have this for a dollar? It's plaster, I think, but I like it."

His head dropped, and she handed him a bill from her pocket.

He didn't take it.

Maybe he was drunk.

She left the dollar on the table, weighed down by an old machine part.

SUNDAY

As Daisy came through the turnstile, she saw a dealer point her out to a man who approached her.

He was a New York City police detective. "Were you here yesterday morning?" he asked.

"Yes!"

"About this time?"

"Yes."

"Would you mind answering some questions?"

Detective Taig was tall with rough dark hair, green eyes, and a deep voice. He was standing by the table next to the gate. Daisy's dollar was still there under the machine part. The TV tray and tarp-tent were still there, too.

"How did you get here?" he asked.

"Subway."

"The IRT?"

"How did you know?"

"You came from that direction."

"Ha, ha, ha," she laughed.

"How did you get here?"

"What?"

"From Twenty-Eighth or Twenty-Seventh Street."

"I thought you were trying to trick me!"

As a sculptor, she charmed wood and stone. On people, too, she tried to leave a mark.

"You were at this booth?"

"I found a little cup I liked, and bought it."

"Who did you buy it from?"

"There was a man in that chair. I said, 'You must be frozen!' Is he dead?"

"You said you bought something from him."

"I asked him if the cup was a dollar, and he nodded. That's important."

"Why?"

"Rigor mortis hadn't set in."

"Okay."

"I read murder mysteries," she added, laughing.

"I'd like to borrow the cup you bought."

Daisy didn't see the point. You'll lose it, she thought, but gave him her name and address.

"You'll get it back."

"I'm freezing. I haven't had a chance to look around yet."

Then she stumped across the lot, her face frozen in a grimace, wondering what to do.

"I hope you didn't mind me putting the fuzz on you," said the dealer who'd pointed her out.

AT HOME, Daisy opened her closet and took out a small white porcelain cup.

She put the blue cup from the dead dealer in its place.

The closet was for things still under consideration. Once she decided to keep something, it went into a six-foot-tall china cabinet against the wall by the door. It was flanked by two mahogany sculpture stands, the bench screws removed. The bench screws with her chisels, rasps, and mallets, wiped and brushed clean, were locked up in her tool chest.

Daisy didn't mind giving the police *something* but wasn't done looking at the blue cup yet.

She went to her kitchen and washed her new purchases. She hadn't found much today—a white oval platter and a tiny glass doll—and was enjoying the warm water when her bell rang.

"Who is it?" she called on her way to the door.

"Detective Taig."

She saw him through the peephole and slowly turned the lock.

"Here's the cup," she said. "It's cracked, so be careful with it."

"Everything wonderful is a little cracked," Taig said. "Emerson said that."

She couldn't hide her amazement that he even knew that name.

MONDAY

"Did you know a dealer was stabbed to death at your flea market?"
"I thought he froze!"
"It's in the papers," Daphne Kodaly said. "Should I read it to you?"
"No, I'll go down and buy it."

A HOMELESS man was pointing to a powdered donut in the bakery window.

Daisy knew how he felt, so when she bought it for him she made sure it was the right one.

Carrying a roll, coffee, the *Times*, the *Post*, and cigarettes, she went back up to her apartment.

MURDER AT THE FLEA MARKET
A 66-year-old African-American man, Jim Luckey, was found murdered in his booth at the Twenty-Sixth Street flea market on Saturday.

"Someone didn't like his prices," Richard Smith, another dealer, said.

Mr. Luckey arrived at the parking lot "before 6 a.m.," according to manager Ray Ho. There, Mr. Luckey unloaded the household furnishings and tools he hoped to sell that day.

At 4 p.m., the dealers were loading their vans for the long drive home. It was an old-fashioned scene of activity at dusk on one of the coldest days of the year.

Cheerful cries of "Let's get moving" were ignored by Mr. Luckey.

Mr. Ho, known as "the man with the clipboard," informed Mr. Luckey that the lot was closing.

As customers and dealers realized that he was dead, some wept. Others said they thought it was a good way to go. But that was before police ruled the case a homicide.

The market was sparsely attended by dealers and customers.

"It was so cold, you didn't want to blink in case it made a breeze," Eddie Kowalski, a dealer, said.

"I guess life is cheap at the flea market," a woman carrying a wooden pedestal remarked. "I'll probably think of that every time I look at this."

Daisy knew both dealers. She had bought an album of tintypes from Richard Smith. Eddie Kowalski was Mr. Flea.

She cut out the articles and read them over, enjoying her coffee.

SATURDAY

"How much is this?"

Daisy held up a little mother-of-pearl jackknife and saw that the other side was cracked.

"Two dollars."

At least the dealer didn't say "That's a miniature" or "Those are collectible."

She paid.

At the last booth she came to, she saw a familiar machine part.

"Can you use that?" asked a young African-American man. "You must be an artist if you can find a use for that."

"I thought I saw it in the booth of the man who was killed here."

"He was my father."

"I think he was a hero," she said warmly. "I think all the dealers here are heroes."

"Why, thank you."

"You make it possible for us to find the things we love. It must have been great having a father who liked old things."

The man smiled but didn't answer.

"It's been hard," he said. "I appreciate you being nice, but people are just vultures, you know? Dad was all excited about some old cup. Took it uptown and at first they said, nah, it's nothing much and offered him twenty bucks. And he figures maybe he can do just as well here, right?"

"Right! Which shop?"

"Don't know. Just up on Madison. And they yammer, yammer, he talks them up and a deal is done—good, right? Not good when he hears it's going to a museum for money that would have changed his life."

"I am so sorry."

"And then it all ended like this.

"And his barn? Way upstate? I went there after the funeral and it was ransacked. Figure somebody heard he was being buried and decided to go loot his things. I'm just trying to sell off what's left.

"People, man. I see now why Dad preferred old stuff to the human race."

BACK IN her neighborhood, Daisy picked up a sandwich from the coffee shop before going up to her apartment.

She took the blue cup out of the closet. None of her books showed anything like the x or y impression on the cup's foot.

Daisy dug at a white spot on the cup with the tip of a razor and didn't even scratch it. The cup was stoneware.

The handle was a snake. It had eyes, nostrils, a mouth, and two indentations on either side of the tail. His jaw was pressed to the wall of the cup near the top facing down, and his body looped around, belly up. The back of his tail was pressed down near the base.

"Biting Snake" handles, adapted from dragons, started around 1750, she had read. Her snake was so much plainer, she wondered if it could be older than that.

"Who are you?" she wondered.

Somehow, Daisy believed, she had the stolen Elers cup.

In *The Soul of Things*, published in 1863, William Denton said psychics saw the scenes imprinted on objects. Daisy believed that was possible, that objects photographed their surroundings.

She had called her sculptures Witnesses because they watched and recorded her struggles.

Daisy put the cup to her forehead and closed her eyes.

SUNDAY

Happy to have a date with Daphne, Daisy walked down to Twenty-Third Street, passed the soot-sprinkled casts in the window, and opened the door of the Sculpture Shop.

"Hi, Bruce!"

"Where have you been?" he asked.

Daisy had been coming to the shop for at least thirty years and had known Bruce all that time. Daphne hoped being there would inspire Daisy to start working again.

The two Gaston Lachaise bronzes were on a worktable, and they were already discussing the bases.

"How about pure white marble?" Daphne asked Daisy. "Bruce said he'd make the tops slightly convex."

"That would be brilliant!" Daisy enthused.

They didn't need Daisy, so she walked around followed by two art students.

"Are you Daisy Summerfield?"

"Yes. Hi."

"Bronico wouldn't let us in to hear you speak."

"I'll talk to your class someday."

She stopped to look at tools, a Dremel and Pow-R-Tron, tempted to buy something.

"What have you been doing?" Bruce asked her.

"Nothing much."

"Well, don't be a stranger."

WHEN THEY got outside, Daphne gave her a clipping from the day's paper.

BULL IN A CHINA SHOP

To the Editor: I was interested enough in your story on the theft of a unique Elers cup to look up more information.

"British Craftsman," London, 1948, shows a cup "probably by Elers," c. 1695, so the stolen cup could not possibly be "the only one of its kind."

Also, there is a photograph of an Elers teapot, c. 1750. Your article says their factory closed in 1700.

Is it too much to hope for experts to get their facts straight?

Larry Finkelstein
Brooklyn, N.Y.

Daisy kissed the newsprint.

"I've made my choice. I will be Mrs. Larry Finkelstein."

Daphne laughed, aghast.

"I need a bathrobe," she said. "Will you go to Lord & Taylor with me?"

LOOKING THROUGH the racks, Daisy found the only good robe—it was a cream-colored, man-tailored Viyella robe dotted with tiny lavender, blue, and pink flowers—and pulled it off the rack.

"That's not your size."

A saleswoman tried to take it from her.

"Do you have it in her size?"

"I'll see."

When she left, Daisy said, "Try it on," and held Daphne's coat and bag.

The sleeves were too long and the hemline touched the floor. Daisy would have rolled up the sleeves and worn it that way.

She said, "It's prettier big. That's how they'd show it in *Elle*."

They didn't have it in a smaller size.

Daphne said she'd take it.

As the saleswoman wrote it up, Daisy flicked a ballpoint pen to the floor before the robe could touch it.

At last it was folded in tissue paper and placed inside a shopping bag.

Daphne carried it jauntily onto the escalator.

It was a surprisingly warm and beautiful day, so they walked uptown.

"What did you tell the students beside the Gettysburg Address?" Daphne asked.

"It isn't like the lectures you give. I don't have slides. I just sit and talk."

"They must love it," Daphne said. "I wish I had been there."

Daphne was worried about Daisy. She hadn't had a show in four years. She must have money socked away, but what would happen in the future?

Daphne didn't think she had been seeing anyone since she broke up with Joe De Leo. Aside from going to the flea market, she didn't know what Daisy did with herself.

"I think," Daphne said, "you should borrow one of your Witnesses from the gallery. It might inspire you to pick up where you left off."

Daisy wished she had gone to the flea market and bought something to look at when she got home. Things she bought were poor substitutes for her work, but they tided her over.

She thought of the blue cup.

"Do you think you could get me Leon Rose's address? I'd love to send him a card."

"Oh, that's nice!" Daphne said. "I'll call you with it tonight."

MONDAY

"No one would believe you anyway, so there's no harm in blabbing," Leon told Daisy, smiling shyly.

Daisy hadn't told Daphne the real reason she wanted Leon's address. Daphne would have been horrified. Besides, Daisy had no plan. To her amazement, Leon admitted what he'd done right away.

"I liked Mr. Luckey and I felt bad for him," Leon continued. "I called him anonymously, you know, because I felt bad. He came back to the shop but my father said all sales are final and threatened to call the police. Mr. Luckey was, well, a bit raggedy, so who would take his side?

"A terrible thing," Leon said. "You heard he was murdered?"

"Yes," Daisy said.

Leon shook his head.

"When the cup went, *ahem*, missing, father was convinced Mr. Luckey stole it. Even though it happened when we all were there. Almost literally under his nose."

Leon paused for dramatic effect.

"I took it," he said.

"Is that why your father was angry at you that day?"

Leon looked surprised she knew that. "Oh, no! Heavens! He didn't know and still doesn't and I will deny everything."

"I'm on your side!" Daisy exclaimed.

"Well, thank you. I told my father I was quitting. That's why he was upset. I pretended I was inconsolable about the loss of the cup. I left there with it in my pocket sweating bullets. Very early Saturday, in the freezing cold, I waited for a chance to return the cup to Mr. Luckey's booth.

"I debated just handing it back but got cold feet, literally and figuratively. I was afraid of how he'd react. I thought, correctly, I could sneak it in among the other things. Then I planned to call him and tell him anonymously, like before.

"I'd say something clever like, 'Not all sales are final. Check your stock. Booyah!'"

"And someone killed Jim Luckey."

"Was the murder related to—all this other business? I can only hope not. I don't suppose we'll ever know.

"Thank you, Ms. Summerfield. It feels good to tell all this to someone. I just wish I knew if I ended up making a bad situation so much worse."

DAISY WAS having the most fun since she stopped working. She often longed for a normal life, she envied waiters, professors—anyone with a job.

And she was sure that is what this was like! Rather than straining over things that were impossible, being a detective was just deciding what was possible.

What kind of person could commit murder at the flea market?

It would have to be someone she couldn't possibly like.

DAISY GOT off the bus on the east side of Fifth Avenue, and crossed back to the museum side.

She walked along the cobbles and then beside the empty fountain.

Daisy was climbing the steps when she remembered it was Monday, the art world's day of rest.

Offices and the gift shop were still open and tourists could come in and get warm. So she climbed to the top, entered the Great Hall, and found a seat facing the door.

A baby wearing the bottom half of a pink snowsuit was banging on the bench near her.

"Stop it," thought Daisy.

The toddler and her parents lived in the city and the grandparents were visiting.

The young woman spoke angrily to her mother-in-law while the two men sat humbly.

Daisy saw them as a family of potters who had made the little pot.

She opened her coat, loosened her scarf, and opened Volume 2 of *Pottery and Porcelain* by Warren E. Cox as she waited for John Lorimer.

For those who think this world is a shadow, old books on china were written. The prose is lapidary. There's humor. There's passion. You think you see what the author is saying, but you are in a dark cistern.

She looked up Elers in the index, went to the page, and read, "Yet with all the talk of them there is not one piece which can surely be attributed to them."

> They had used the lathe. They had or had not used molds according to the authority whose word you wish to believe.
> But they certainly did not add one jot to the art of ceramics.

Daisy burst out laughing. Josiah Wedgwood, at least, had credited the Elerses with bringing salt glaze to England.

Near her on the bench was a South Asian woman wearing a green-and-gold sari.

Lonely wanderers, like old ceramic pieces. Made by human hands, they roamed the world, sustaining chips and cracks.

Unable to be touched in museum cases, they lose their reason for being.

She thought that might be why some homeless people avoid shelters. "We are all homeless," she thought. Made by an unknown creator, we roam the earth, getting chipped and cracked.

SHE GAVE up on her stakeout and walked home through Central Park, wondering why Cox had said that porcelain was named for the "purple fish" or "Venus shell."

She'd always heard the Italians called it *porcellana*, the word for cowrie shells.

Like many artists, Daisy collected shells and knew something about them.

Cypraea tigris, the tiger cowrie, and *Cypraea aurantium*, the golden cowrie, were good for teething.

She received odd looks when she gave tiger cowries as baby presents.

Daisy stopped and looked back at the museum.

She had started to piece together a picture of the man.

Lorimer had earned his BFA, MFA, and PhD, and become an assistant Decorative Arts curator at the Met years ago.

His boss died, and Lorimer got the job. No one wanted to cross him, even then.

He was unusual in that he liked all the museum departments and attended their social events.

Artists gave him their work, hoping that influential people would see it.

They weren't disappointed.

He talked about "his" artists and helped to arrange exhibits and purchases.

The nastiness under his charm was like catnip to these artists.

Now, somewhere in the museum, John Lorimer might think he'd gotten away with murder.

TUESDAY

As Daisy stood at the Junior Museum Entrance, a fur coat passed. It was John Lorimer. He was crossing Fifth Avenue.

"What a walk," she thought, following him east on Eighty-First Street.

Lorimer didn't move his upper body or his hips, and he toed out slightly.

He turned uptown on Madison, and when he came to the coffee shop on the southeast corner of Eighty-Second Street, he opened the door and went in.

She thought they would eat at a small French restaurant.

He took a seat at the counter and Daisy chose a stool a few seats down. She took out a book, *Kitty Carter, Canteen Girl*.

AFTER FINISHING his turkey on whole wheat ("mayonnaise on the side"), Lorimer went to the front to pay his bill. Daisy slowly followed, tying her scarf.

He left and she followed him down the west side of Madison.

He stopped, waited for the light, crossed the avenue, and went down to James Rose.

Daisy strained her eyes but didn't see him press the bell before he went in.

She started to cross Madison, changed her mind, and started downtown.

What was she doing really?

A passage in *Kitty Carter* (published by Whitman in 1944) had struck her:

> She thought bitterly of what her psychology teacher had said about how human beings compensate for losses and disappointments. Yes, that was exactly what she was trying to do in making herself a private secret-service agent. She imagined she could do something big enough in uncovering some dastardly plot against her country. This would compensate for her not being able to do more to help the war effort.

Was she like Kitty, canteen girl? Was Daisy trying to compensate for her own loss?

Daisy started walking downtown again, turned west, and crossed Fifth Avenue. Soon the Kodaly Gallery appeared on her right.

A new receptionist was at the desk.

"Hi," Daisy said. "Will you ask Alan if I can see him? My name is Daisy Summerfield."

"Is he expecting you?"

"I'm one of your artists."

Someone was coming up the stairs.

"Hi, Daisy," Melanie Lefkowitz, an assistant curator, said. "Does Alan know you're here?"

He appeared and Daisy felt his tie against her cheek and breathed in his cologne.

He said, "I thought I heard your voice! Why aren't you sculpting pickle dishes?"

They walked down the hall to his office. The remains of his lunch were on his desk.

Two of her Witnesses were on the mantel.

"Are they the only two you have left?"

He said, "I think there are two more."

"I'd like to borrow one sometime. Daphne suggested it."

"I think that's a good idea," he said. "Artists should live with their work."

"And I had an idea for a show."

"Tell me your idea."

The receptionist came in and told Alan he had a call from Amsterdam.

Hearing him speak Dutch, it seemed to her that things had not changed much since the Renaissance, when artists had rich and cultured patrons.

He hung up, left the room, came back, and said, "We have four Witnesses. Two are in storage. Now tell me your idea."

"You know I love the flea market. All artists do. Look at all the things Rembrandt bought at auction!"

He must have bought china, she realized. She would check the 1656 Inventory in *Rembrandt and the Italian Renaissance* by Kenneth Clark, when she got home. Due to the way small pieces of china travel, it would be possible to own something from Rembrandt's china collection.

"Of course he paid top prices. He said he did it for the dignity of his profession." Daisy laughed.

"Most artists don't have money, but they set the styles for what people want. The show could be things artists found.

"Some could be for sale. The price and where and when they found it would be part of the art. You could sell a Henry Moore maquette someone paid ten dollars for, for I don't know how much."

He beamed at her. "Did you find a Henry Moore maquette?"

"No, but it's something I could find."

Alan thought about it. "We can do it in summer," he mused. "No one wants to have a solo show in summer."

"May I curate it?"

"Of course! It's your vision."

"Great!"

"How about the portrait?"

"You know I saw John Lorimer leave James Rose after the robbery. He was wearing a fur coat. I told him he was insane."

Alan had a high-pitched laugh that ended, "Oh my God."

"I saw him go there today," she said, laughing, too.

"What were you doing there?"

"I think Lorimer is a murderer. I think I have the Elers cup, but I won't put it in the show if I'm the curator."

"Daisy, could you say that again, please?"

ALAN TOOK it well, all in all, though he had a hard time believing a Decorative Arts curator at the Met could ever do such a thing. Still, he was concerned that Daisy thought that following him around was a good idea.

"Go to the police!" he'd said.

"With what? Of course the cup might have Lorimer's fingerprints but what would that prove? He would have handled it with James Rose."

That evening, Daisy's parents called from Florida. She said, "I may curate a show at the Kodaly Gallery."

"You better not!" her father said. "You don't know the first thing about catering."

Then Daphne called.

"Daisy," she said with worry in her voice, "you need to drop this."

"Why?"

"Because John may try to hurt you."

"Physically?"

"No, professionally. And Alan said you think you have the stolen cup. You need to go to the police! I believe you're a great artist, but making sculpture and solving crimes are two different things."

"They're not! Degas said making art was like committing a crime."

"I think he meant that colors that were changed, things painted out, hands and feet hidden. Taking space and perspective from Japanese woodcuts or twisting a clay horse into a bathing woman," Daphne said. "Not being an actual criminal!"

"I really want to solve this! A dealer was killed at *my* flea market!" Daisy said.

"You read too many murder mysteries. This could be dangerous."

"It's not a mystery. I know who did it. I care that a dealer was killed. He was nice!" At least, unlike other rude dealers, he had been clinically dead.

"Daisy, call the police."

"They'd do nothing but take my cup and I'd never see it again!"

WEDNESDAY

Daisy was studying a porcelain greyhound.

Three of his paws and his tail were missing. One lovely up-turned back paw remained. He had pale blue spots under the glaze. His silver-gray eyes, nose, mouth, and collar, very thin and fine, were also under the glaze.

He was stamped "CP," the *P* within the *C*, on the unglazed, or bisque, or biscuit bottom.

The dog looked French.

Cox listed "CP," as a French mark, Charles Philippe, 1773, but she couldn't find it with the *P* inside the *C*.

She gave it up.

Daphne's concern had rattled her. What if Lorimer did try to harm her?

She went to her tool chest, removed the china from the top, unlocked it, raised the lid, and saw her carving tools.

They were all so familiar, every nick, spot, and maker's mark on them.

Her fingers curled into positions to hold them.

Why did she care about porcelain dogs?

She took out a mallet and relocked the chest.

She couldn't call the police. She had given the detective the wrong cup.

"Tell him you made a mistake," she thought. "Call Information, get the number for the Chelsea precinct, and ask for Detective Taig."

It was sweet, his quoting Emerson. Sympathy flooded her heart.

But what was she thinking? She couldn't give up the cup!

The phone rang.

"Hello?"

"This is John Lorimer."

"Hi!"

"I demand to know why you were following me. I assume your 'sculptor's block' has unhinged you."

"I needed background for your portrait."

"I don't want you to do my portrait."

"Well, I don't want to do it!" Daisy said, surprised his rejection hurt.

"Two of your sculptures are in our Modern collection. I can have them de-accessioned."

"I know you killed Jim Luckey. I think he just made you really, really angry. He was better than you and found something more beautiful than you ever did."

There was a long pause.

"Please deposit for the next three minutes, or your call will be interrupted."

"You're at a pay phone?"

"Surprised?"

"No. You don't want the call traced. Should I call you back?"

A coin dropped.

"A knife can be a great work of art. Chances are you'll be buying one."

He hung up.

"TAIG," THE detective said.

"I met you at the flea market when a dealer was killed. I thought he froze!"

"Okay."

"Something happened tonight that's related to it."

She read him her notes, leaving out that she gave him the wrong cup.

The conversation didn't go as Daisy had hoped.

The detective clearly thought it was impossible that a Decorative Arts curator threatened her life. But Taig did promise to question Lorimer when he could.

THURSDAY

Daisy was scared to go out for coffee. It was past noon and her head ached.

Her phone rang.

She snatched it up.

Daphne said, "I was opening the mail at the gallery and found this: 'Tell your friend to mind her own business or she'll get hurt.'"

"Are the letters cut out of magazines?"

"What?"

"How is it written?"

"It's typed."

"Do you have a plastic bag?"

"Wait, Daisy—"

"Put it and the envelope in a plastic bag. Use a tissue. Hold them by the corners."

"Daisy, I made it up! I was just trying to get you to stop."

Daisy didn't believe her. She would go to the gallery and find the letter.

"Okay," she said. "You got me. Hey, you suggested I should borrow one of my Witnesses here. Alan said it was okay."

"Do you know which one?"

"No. Two are in storage. Will you ask Melanie to take them out for me?"

"Don't come today. Alan and I have to leave at three."

"Perfect," thought Daisy.

LATER THAT afternoon Daisy carefully checked the street and got out of a west-bound cab across from her apartment building. She was carrying one of her sculptures, a gray, pink, and mica-speckled Witness, eighteen inches tall.

While Melanie took out her unsold work, Daisy searched Daphne's desk but didn't find a letter. Disappointed, she took the Witness and headed nervously back home.

She had her *lignum vitae* mallet with her for protection.

But when someone roughly grabbed her arm, the mallet was in her coat pocket.

Daisy turned and instinctively raised her tall granite sculpture to protect it.

The granite connected with her attacker's soft chin.

"Call the police," Daisy told neighbors, who were walking around Lorimer to get into the building.

They nodded in a noncommittal New Yorker way, but she soon heard sirens, and three police cars pulled up. A young officer asked her what had happened.

"He attacked me."

"How?"

"Give me your money," she growled.

They looked down at Lorimer in his glossy fur coat.

The officer opened his notebook.

Other officers stood around.

"Did anyone see what went down?" the first one asked the small crowd that gathered.

"I saw it all," a mentally ill woman said. "He pulled a gun on her. She kicked it out of his hand, caught it, spun around, and hit him with it."

She smiled, showing toothless gums.

As Daisy smiled back at her, she heard an ambulance wailing and beeping up Broadway.

An older officer said, "What happened?"

"He"—she pointed with the toe of her gold-colored work boot— "grabbed my arm. He scared me."

The sight of her own boot and the worn hem of her jeans reassured her.

"Do you know him?"

"No! He jerked my arm and my sculpture hit him."

"Whoa," the officer said, taking it from her.

It was dark. The rotating lights hurt her eyes, and she heard buzzing.

One of the building's new tenants came outside, and she thought, "I bet he's a young lawyer." But he put his hand on the elevator man's arm and asked, "Would you mind taking us up?"

Before he left, the elevator man winked at her.

She was surprised to see her neighbors leave the scene. She would always stop to watch a sidewalk drama.

Now paramedics were moving Lorimer onto a stretcher. A thin gold watch gleamed at his wrist when his arm fell over the side before they strapped him in.

They raised the stretcher and wheeled it away. Something shone on the sidewalk.

"Is that a knife?" Daisy asked, going toward it.

An officer picked it up and wouldn't answer.

The first officer returned from the ambulance. Two paramedics got in, and it left.

Two officers followed it in their police car.

Two more officers got into another blue-and-white and slammed the doors.

The deranged woman had gone.

"What is that?" the young cop asked the older one.

"It's a sculpture," said Daisy.

"Here, catch," the older cop said, grinning.

"Careful!" she cried.

"What is it, a rock?"

"It's granite. If it falls, it will crack."

A pain sliced through her.

"You hit the guy with this?"

"It was an accident. That sculpture is insured for two hundred thousand dollars."

"So what is it, ott?" he asked in the accent of an outer borough.

"Yes. May I go up?"

"We're taking this with us."

She started to protest.

"We'll be careful," the older cop told her.

He turned a page in his notebook, and, for the second time that month, she watched a police officer take down her name and address.

"YOU WERE great." The elevator man hugged Daisy. "Are you all right?"

"I'm fine, thanks, Modesto."

After she unlocked her door, went inside, and took the mallet out of her pocket, she called Detective Taig.

"I met you at the flea market—" she began.

"Yes, Ms. Summerfield, I remember."

Daisy hoped he believed her now but, at the moment, was far more concerned about her sculpture.

"My work has value. I was bringing it home from my gallery."

"I promise you, I'll look into everything," Taig said.

FRIDAY

Taig called surprisingly early.

"Ms. Summerfield? Detective Taig. Good news."

Mayor's Award! She didn't know what to wear.

"Dr. Lorimer says he won't press charges if you don't. He says he knows you. He saw you on the street and wanted to say hello."

"What was he doing in my neighborhood?"

"Going to see friends."

"Who weren't expecting him."

Taig grunted.

"And he had a knife?"

"Lorimer said he had it as a work of art. It was very ornate. And totally clean. No connection to the Jim Luckey murder, which still seems ridiculous but I did have it checked."

"He was going to kill me!"

"Hey, hey, I'm taking this seriously, but I'm sorry. It's your word against his. You told an officer he asked you for money. And that hitting him was an accident."

"I didn't know what to say!"

"You can pick up your sculpture at the precinct."

"Thank you," she said stiffly. "Oh, and I want the cup I gave you back, too!"

"I wanted to catch a killer," she told her walls after she hung up.

DAISY WAS back, sitting in the office of the president of the Kodaly Gallery.

"I heard this morning that Lorimer is leaving the museum and going to a gallery in Sydney, Australia," Alan said, concern for her in his eyes.

She had taken up a lot of his time. The phone flashed nonstop, and he ignored it.

Suddenly, she felt happy. "I thought they found the cup at the flea market, and I was upset I didn't find it, but I did find it at the flea market."

"Yes, you did," Alan Kodaly said so warmly, she had to look away.

Her delicate features fell into lines old and grave. "I apologize if I hurt you or the gallery."

"Not at all!" he said. "I asked if you wanted to give the world a picture of a Decorative Arts curator and that's what you did."

She smiled.

"Oh!" she said. "Do you know what kind of solvent works best on stoneware?"

SUMMER, LATER THAT YEAR

The show at the Kodaly Gallery, "Artists Go Shopping," was a hit with critics and the public.

The centerpiece of the show, curated by Daisy Summerfield, was an Elers cup credited as the find of Jim Luckey.

James Rose added drama when he claimed it was the same cup stolen from his shop in January. The cup in the Summerfield show, however, was plain white stoneware, not blue.

The cup was later sold by Jim Luckey's son to China's Shanghai Museum for their new gallery of British *chinoiserie* entitled, 他们尽力而为, which translates roughly as "They did their best."

Death Goes Dutch

1990

SATURDAY

I t was a hot summer day.

Daisy was on the phone with Daphne Kodaly while looking at a small *blanc de chine* bowl she bought at the flea market.

"Who?" she asked Daphne.

"James and Bunny Six."

"Are they any relation to Jan Six, friend of Rembrandt?"

Holding the bowl to the light, she saw a grayish translucency.

A raised branch of five plum blossoms looped across the front. One large blossom was incised on the back.

"They collect nineteenth-century horse paintings that will go to Yale."

"Are they in country day school now?"

"Who?"

"The horses."

"Ah," Daphne said. "The Sixes had some china stolen, and Alan told them you could find it!"

"I'd love to!"

"Alan was joking."

Artists, like cats, are hunters and loungers. They need silence to hear, space to see, and no timetable.

In seconds these daredevils can perform amazing feats—or an embarrassing fiasco.

Like felines, artists need praise. They need to know they're admired.

"Where do they live?" asked Daisy.

Books say you can gently dissuade cats from doing things you don't want them to do.

"Northern Westchester. You'd have to take the train and wear a dress."

SUNDAY

Seeing a large set of Fiestaware at the flea market made Daisy melancholy.

The light blue was her favorite, but all the colors were old friends.

"Where's the light blue?" she asked.

"The turquoise?" came the dealer's squeaky voice. "That was the sixth color, in 1937. This is the original 1936 set with five colors."

"I never liked the white."

"The ivory?"

"I don't think our family had it."

Up and down the aisles she went, searching for a rare old piece of china.

She entered a booth and saw an all-white water dropper shaped like a gourd. It had a raised flower, a raised vine, and a three-dimensional bird.

She picked it up and turned it over. The numerals "9-9" were inscribed on the base.

She had one like it with an incised triangle and an *N* or a *Z*.

The feet weren't as beautiful as the ones on hers, she thought, setting it down.

She picked it up again.

"How much is this?" she asked a large woman wearing a sun hat on her orange hair.

"Eight."

"I have one like it."

"It's Chinese," the sweating haystack said.

"Can you make it less?"

"Six."

"I paid five for mine." Daisy remembered she had bought it from this same woman.

"Do you have any more?" Daisy asked, picturing a carton of these water droppers.

"I wish I did!"

She paid for the water dropper and now had two of what had once been a treasure. She could imagine putting them both in a shopping bag and giving them to a thrift shop.

Daisy looked on all the tables. Everything in the blinding sunlight suddenly seemed suspect to her.

Nothing tempted her.

Everywhere she looked, she saw deranged people lying and bragging over dirty old objects.

She saw someone beautiful seated in a lawn chair. As she gazed at the person to refresh her eyes, she saw it was a cocker spaniel.

Even Mr. Flea wasn't a happy sight. There was an addition to his booth since last summer, a newsprint photo of the crowd at the "Artists Go Shopping" show. Mr. Flea was among the Upper East Side crowd. It depressed her because, with hindsight, Daisy wished she'd asked him to have a booth at the show.

She crossed Sixth Avenue and walked down to Twenty-Third Street and bought a carton of juice and a small bag of vinegar-and-salt potato chips.

Then she walked slowly to the subway on the downtown shady side of the street. At Seventh Avenue she put the containers in a trash basket and started down the steps, but too many people were coming up, and some were saying, "No service."

She walked back to Sixth Avenue and waited for the Number Five bus.

DAISY TOOK the two water droppers to her desk and stood them side by side.

The new one was an eighth of an inch shorter. Clay shrinks when fired, so a copy made from a mold would be smaller than the original.

In some ways the second water dropper was finer. It had more detail, but overall it wasn't as pleasing.

Plate 65 B. in *Blanc de Chine* by P. J. Donnelly showed a Chinese water dropper that might have been a pattern for hers.

Her phone rang and broke her concentration.

"Come to tea!" cried Bunny Six.

"I'd love to!" said Daisy.

She'd had tea every day for two weeks at the Mountbatten Hotel in London, while listening to a harpist.

WEDNESDAY

On the Metro-North train rattling north, Daisy was wearing a new dress, an oversize ankle-length cotton jersey.

Trees, the backs of houses, a stonecutter's yard, and other sights went by.

Daisy opened an old paperback she'd found at the flea market, *Faidoh Lorraine and the Spectator* by Thomas Garfield.

> Jane Lorraine glided on high heels out the door of the bungalow.
>
> A pair of feet in brown-and-white spectator pumps stuck out of a shrub beside the front door.
>
> "Oh, Faidoh," she called to her brother, "you've got company!"
>
> She continued down the walk, sprang into her old DeSoto, and drove to the drugstore to meet her best friend, Carole Camell.

"Sorry I'm late," she said breathlessly.

Jane ordered coffee and a hot roast-beef sandwich with gravy.

Carole ordered milk, and a bacon, lettuce, and tomato sandwich.

When the admiring waiter had gone, Jane said, "There's a dead body in front of our house."

Carole asked, "Remember the delivery man?" [*Faidoh Lorraine and the Package*]

"Yes," answered Jane, "and the door-to-door salesman." [*Faidoh Lorraine and the Bible*]

They wondered who it could be this time!

"Horsefly!" the conductor called.

Meanwhile, Faidoh Lorraine was examining the corpse's footwear and wondering the same thing.

There were taps on the toes of the worn leather soles. He noted the small economy.

Daisy put the book away. A few people were on the platform. An equally small group of passengers got off the train.

She recognized one of them.

"Detective Taig! Hi. I'm Daisy Summerfield. Do you remember me?"

"Yes, it's good to see you."

"Thank you. I'm still alive, as you can see."

"It's good to see that, too."

Were they working the same case?

"I'm surprised they called you in from New York."

"It's my pleasure."

They climbed the concrete steps, crossed over the tracks, and went down.

A handsome woman wearing ancient shorts and a sleeveless blouse came up to Daisy.

"I just saw your mother," she told Taig, and didn't wait for a response.

"I have to make one stop," the woman said, when she and Daisy were seated in her stifling hot car.

Bunny Six drove across the street, pulled into a slot in front of a deli, and said, "Wait here."

She faced a row of three-story Victorian buildings.

No antiques shop, no junk shop that Daisy could see.

Bunny came out and handed Daisy a small brown bag, which she put on the floor.

"I thought Detective Taig was coming."

"No such luck," Bunny said.

They drove down a country road. Daisy saw trees and horses, but she smelled corned beef.

The house was as big as a castle.

"Where did you go to school?" Bunny asked.

"Dewey."

"What year were you?"

"Sixty-two."

"I was in the class of '40, but I left to marry James."

"I went to New York," Daisy said as they walked down a flag-stone hall.

Paintings by George Stubbs were on the walls, and a man sat reading a paper in the dining room.

"Sit down," Bunny said. "I'll get a plate for your sandwich."

"I'm sorry, I don't eat meat!"

"I thought you were Jewish. You can have Daisy's sandwich," Bunny said to the man, and Daisy handed him the grease-spotted bag.

He uncrossed his long legs, and she saw he wasn't wearing socks.

"What kind of china was stolen?" she asked.

"It was white, yellow, green, orange, and blue."

"Gaudy Dutch?" asked Daisy.

Bunny turned to the man who strongly resembled Cézanne's gardener, Vallier.

Daisy trusted her own instincts so well, she realized he was Bunny's gardener.

"Mebbe," he said, glancing up.

She wasn't a snob. Why didn't she tell him her name and hold out her hand?

"Artists are true aristocrats," she thought proudly.

Bunny went through a swinging door and the gardener took his sandwich and paper and followed her, leaving Daisy alone with her elbows on the dented walnut table.

She had often been in homes like this for, in buying contemporary art, collectors thought they bought the artist as well.

Daisy felt something sticky and lifted her elbows. The table's grimy surface pulled at the sleeves of her pale green dress.

The table left dark smudges on her elbows. She hit and brushed them with her hand.

She looked at pea-green walls, a cream-colored ceiling, and mahogany sideboard.

It was a beautiful room, plain and spacious.

She noticed a wall that might be one side of a built-in china cabinet, and got up to look. The set inside looked like Royal Swansea and nothing seemed to be missing from the shelves.

Daisy knocked on the swinging door and entered a kitchen that dated from the forties.

An open package was on the counter. "May I have a cookie?" she asked.

"Help yourself."

DAISY GUESSED the Sixes' stolen china was Gaudy Dutch from the colors and because rich people collected it.

Back in her apartment, sitting on her oak parquet floor, she looked at her five books by Sam Laidacker.

"The colors used are blue, green, reddish-orange, and yellow with a reddish-brown rim," she read.

This name is given because it is found chiefly among the Pennsylvania Dutch or in sections to which they migrated. At first it was thought to have been made in the lower counties of Pennsylvania but is now generally believed to have been made in England for the Pennsylvania Dutch trade.

Daisy knew where to start.

SATURDAY

Daisy went from booth to booth.

At the north end of the Antiques market, on one of three long tables covered with white sheets, Daisy found a Gaudy Dutch cup and saucer.

A label in the cup said "$50."

Daisy held the saucer to the light.

No shadow of her fingers showed through it.

Gaudy Dutch was pottery, not porcelain. It shouldn't be translucent and it wasn't.

A friendly young woman came over to her.

"Can you do any better?" Daisy asked.

"I can do forty-five dollars. That's the Grape pattern."

"Can you make it forty dollars?"

She thought it over and agreed.

"Do you have any more?" Daisy asked, watching her wrap them in newspaper.

"Gaudy Dutch is hard to find," the dealer said. "That's why I priced it so high."

As Daisy took the package from her she saw that a creepy man with jet-black hair and wearing a black raincoat was watching.

She went to the gate just at the right time.

"Detective Taig! I thought we were going to the same place from the train," she told him.

"I guess not."

"Some of the Sixes' china was stolen. I think it was Gaudy Dutch. I want to show you this out-of-print booklet I ordered. Look at these patterns. The thief may sell it here."

"Why here?"

"It's well known, and dealers bring expensive stuff, too," Daisy said. And she was praying she wouldn't have to take the train or ferry to one of the other four boroughs: the Bronx, Brooklyn, Queens, or Staten Island.

"I don't know which pattern they had," Daisy continued, "but they're the same colors. They look like folk art."

"How did you like Horsefly?"

"It's beautiful."

"Yes, it's a good town. My parents live there."

Daisy saw it. He was born on the wrong side of the tracks, smarter than his classmates who went to Ivy League colleges while he went to the police academy.

He probably had all their prejudices with none of their advantages or privileges.

She said, "I found one cup and saucer, but the woman I bought them from isn't a criminal."

Taig smiled. "So are you looking for stolen china or buying it?"

Daisy lowered her voice. "Both." She looked around but didn't see the man with the dyed hair and black raincoat. "Isn't this what you would do undercover? Buy a little and try to find the source?"

"Okay, I understand, I think. But Gaudy Dutch is rare, isn't it?"

How would he know that?

She pictured a rough-haired little boy waiting for his mother to finish work.

"Sit still, sonny. If I drop this Gaudy Dutch, you can kiss the police academy goodbye. We'll be going to the poorhouse."

"Would you like to get some coffee?"

"What?"

The question took her by surprise, but she agreed. Why not?

"Too bad it wasn't Fiestaware," she said, walking down Sixth Avenue with him. "There's a big set back there."

They crossed Twenty-Third Street, ignoring the pretentious cafés that had sprung up in the new professional photography district.

As they cooled off in the air-conditioning of the Fritzie Coffee Shop, he said, "You must like the flea market."

"I love it! Why do people say material things aren't important? They're denigrating the work that goes into them. When I was a girl, we lived on a lake in Minnesota. I'd be in the back seat of our car, thinking, 'I'm the girl who's in this car.'

"That was my identity on the ride to town.

"There was a hardware store in Mound, and my parents would always buy me something. On the way home, I might be the owner of a Princess Elizabeth paper doll. Does that sound familiar?"

"No."

"What about your badge?"

"Just my ID."

"So, nothing important, just your identity?" As she laughed, she saw the man from the flea market sitting at the counter watching her.

"I mean, it doesn't identify me to myself."

Taig reached in his pocket and took out a photo. "Do you know Florence Vito? Ever seen her before?"

"No. Why?"

"She was murdered."

"At the flea market?" It should be her case.

"In her apartment but friends say she was here frequently. She had a lot of china."

"Is any missing?"

"There are two clean circles in the dust."

"That sounds like a poem!"

He smiled at her.

"I'd look at people buying china here," Daisy said. "People who love china are often out of their minds. You should read my books."

SHE WALKED to the downtown end of the platform reading the booklet by Eleanor J. Fox and Edward G. Fox.

Gaudy Dutch designs are not of English origin, though they are no doubt based on imitations of Chinese and Japanese ware manufactured principally in England.

She was already confused.

Ultimately, however, the methods of manufacture and the motifs used in Gaudy Dutch go back to China and Japan.

"Oh, okay."

Though China originated the method of producing "Imari ware," it was not until Japan began to flood the European market with this ware that China copied the method back to make up for the losses it was suffering in European markets because of the demand for Japanese wares.

"What?" she asked the authors. She went to the edge of the platform and looked down the tracks, but saw no white light getting stronger.

What were the motifs that appeared on Chinese and Japanese wares "in the Imari style" imported by the Europeans? The Chinese revered four flowers: Lotus, Cherry Blossom, Peony, and Chrysanthemum.

As she returned to her place at the downtown side of a Lally column, she saw Mr. Black, the man with the dyed hair and raincoat.

She rested her shoulder against the far side of the column, away from him.

The train came. Every seat was taken.

She stayed in front of the door, touching her hip to the arm of the seat next to her.

The train lurched as it started, and she set her feet apart for balance.

Except during rush hours, it is customary for only two people to stand in front of each set of doors. Daisy stood alone.

She reopened the booklet and looked at the garish color photos of the patterns: Butterfly, Carnation, Dahlia, Double Rose, Dove, Grape, Leaf, Oyster, Primrose, Single Rose, Strawflower, Sunflower, Urn, War Bonnet, Zinnia, and No Name.

She liked War Bonnet and Oyster. The black Urn also appealed to her.

Wasn't there a King's Rose, she was wondering, when she felt someone in front of her.

"Go to the other side," she thought irritably.

She moved to the other door. The person went with her.

She felt something hard against her stomach.

An artist looks at everything. Looking down, she thought, "That's not his penis. It's a gun!"

"Give me the cup and saucer," Mr. Black said, killing her with his breath.

"What do I do?" she wondered.

Nine times out of ten, you should read on the subway and avoid the eyes of weirdos. One time in ten, you shouldn't.

"Give me the cup and saucer."

"I'll get it out for you," she said, screwing up her face against his smell.

Mr. Black continued to breathe, and she felt as though she were going to throw up.

Daisy reached into her pocket, found her Acme Thunderer whistle, put it to her lips, and blasted it.

The assailant left.

The train pulled into Seventy-Second Street, the doors opened, and the car emptied.

Daisy pulled the emergency cord and went to the door and blew her whistle.

The doors stayed open and an express train came in.

Should she run across the platform and take it? She could get off at Ninety-Fourth Street.

Ding-dong went the signal. The doors closed. *Ding-dong.* They opened and closed.

The train started to move.

The next stop was Seventy-Ninth Street, a local stop. She thought of a clothes store on Eightieth.

DAISY HAD a gift for finding things to buy. She slipped into Morris Brothers, and saw a white, red, and blue jersey on display.

The front said "NORGES ISHOCKEYFORBUND 18-9-1934" in a circle around a polar bear.

Three red-outlined cowries went across each shoulder. They might have been pucks. They were hexagonal, with a horizontal line through the center.

On the back of the jersey was a player's name, "SKAAR," and his number, "11."

The size was XL.

If a gunman was trying to spot her, it was perfect as a disguise.

Daisy pulled it on over her head, rolled up the sleeves, and gave the tag to the cashier.

She walked home, pleased to have bought the jersey made in Finland.

She loved her time in Helsinki. At first Finnish interiors look drab, but they don't need decoration because everything is so well made.

Daisy thought of getting rid of her desk and buying a tabletop hockey game.

She remembered watching violent games in shoeboxes as a kid. She tried to recall how that went.

No gunman was awaiting her on the brown leatherette sofa inside her lobby.

Pedro took her up with a woman and two miniature poodles who lived across the hall.

AS SHE walked in, her phone rang.

"Where were you?" asked her father.

"The flea market."

"I thought you like to go early, before everything is picked over," her mother said.

Everything was picked over before she woke up. She prided herself on finding things few people knew about.

"Why so late?" she heard her father ask.

She pulled off the jersey and laid it on her bed thinking she should have pearls to wear with it.

"I had coffee with someone."

"Who did you have coffee with?" asked her father.

"Someone from the flea market."

He couldn't believe she was so stupid!

"An accomplice could have come to your apartment with a van and cleaned you out!"

Talking with her parents, Daisy started to feel more normal.

Daphne called next.

"Now I know Bunny didn't call you, or you'd be out getting into trouble," Daphne said.

"She did call and I went out to Horsefly."

"They live on Park Avenue, too, you know."

"Why did you tell me they lived in Horsefly?"

"Because you never go anywhere and I thought you wouldn't start now."

"I found out what kind of china it was. Bunny didn't know, and I had to guess. And today, I found a Gaudy Dutch cup and saucer at the flea market. A man saw me buy it. He followed me to the subway.

"I was standing in front of a door. I know you don't take subways, but this is funny."

"I take subways!"

"Then you know those signs, 'DO NOT LEAN AGAINST THE DOOR.'"

"Of course."

"I was standing in front of a door, reading a book called *Gaudy Dutch*, and he shoved a gun in my stomach and said, 'Give me the cup and saucer.' I thought he was exposing himself!"

"WHAT?"

"Don't you think I looked like a Marsden Hartley painting, with 'NO SE APOYE CONTRA LA PUERTA' above my head and a big black gun in my stomach?"

SATURDAY

Daisy wore her hockey jersey to the flea market and was very happy that dealers didn't recognize her.

At the northernmost booths beside the chain-link fence on Sixth Avenue, there were always small pieces of china.

Daisy reached for a plain white cup decorated with orange, dark blue, green, and luster buds. Inside the bowl, three dark blue panels were set in a field of flowers. The luster turned violet as she revolved it.

"Thees ees a very good cup," the dealer said. "A woman told me eet ees an expensive cup. But eet's missing hees saucer."

"I'll go up to forty," thought Daisy.

"Tree."

The black-haired man was nowhere in sight, and she paid and walked away.

"I HAVEN'T done this in years," Daisy thought, getting a pen and sketchbook.

She drew the ellipse of the Gaudy Dutch cup, then the curved sides, then the straight line of the foot rim on each side, then the curved bottom line.

She started drawing the "grape" cluster, starting with its yellow center.

She drew three half circles around the center, five half circles around those, seven more around the five.

Then she outlined the blue leaf in front of the cluster, making it too large.

She drew another ellipse, then the walls, then the foot.

This time she drew the blue leaf first. "Now my drawing will balance," she thought.

She picked up the cup and examined the painting. First came the colors, then the lines, sure and beautiful.

The cup and saucer had the look of coated paper and the designs were calligraphic. She had read that Gaudy Dutch was sent to America and marketed to the lower classes. How things change.

SUNDAY

Keeping an eye out, Daisy headed toward the flea market's upper lot. It was always interesting there.

Once a family from New Jersey brought paper bags filled with junk. Daisy had knelt on the bumpy hardtop and sorted through it.

Among the things she bought for five dollars that day were a broken necklace of pale pink beads, a tiny cardboard frog whose arms moved on wires, and a brown-flocked plaster rabbit wearing a smooth pink skirt.

Today she stopped at a booth where a woman tried to sell her a gleaming brown jar as Japanese.

There was a small raised bow tie on the belly, and a large bow tie on the bottom. No depictions of Japanese motifs in her books on pottery and porcelain included a bow tie, though it was on British pottery.

"I don't think it's Japanese," Daisy said. "I think it was made in England by someone who admired the Japanese."

"If this is a Bernard Leach studio piece, I'll kill you," the pretty curly-haired dealer told Daisy.

She couldn't wait to take the jar as the dealer wrapped it for her. As Daisy was taking the bag from the dealer, she saw Mr. Black. He didn't seem to have seen her.

No raincoat today, Mr. Black was wearing a Hawaiian-print shirt and Bermuda shorts. His legs above sheer black dress socks were practically hairless.

He must be seventy, she thought.

He was leaving the booth across the aisle, going to the next one down.

The dealer who knew about Bernard Leach studio pieces was helping another customer.

Daisy asked, "Do you know that man in the Hawaiian-print shirt and Bermuda shorts?"

"No."

She stood holding the bag, letting talk of costume jewelry flow over her.

"Is this Miriam Haskell?" someone asked.

She wondered if she should ask the dealer to keep the jar for her, but she was from Massachusetts and didn't come to the flea market every weekend.

Mr. Black was going down the aisle. He was two booths away.

Carrying the jar, Daisy hurried after him. She went to the booth across the aisle and saw two tiny toy cars.

"I can do better on those," a dealer said.

"Thanks! I'll think about them."

Following the black-haired man at a distance, she came to the Famous Attics booth and had to ask.

"Did you sell the Fiestaware?" she asked.

"We've still got it if you want it. We're not selling the pieces separately."

"No?"

"What you saw was eight place settings plus the large serving pieces."

"Wow."

"It came from a wealthy estate. Want it for three hundred dollars?"

She shook her head.

"That's two hundred below book." He showed her the book on Fiestaware.

Looking up from the book, she saw Mr. Black heading for the exit.

She got there in time to hear a dealer scream, "Give me back my tea strainer!"

"I wanted to see it in sunlight."

"Why didn't you ask me?"

"It's no good. The marks are no good."

"What do you mean the marks are no good? No one can fake silver marks!"

Mr. Black gave him back the tea strainer and went out the exit.

Daisy followed him across Twenty-Fifth Street, past the regular flea market.

She saw her old friend Mr. Flea wet his head under the hydrant and get in line for a pita.

AFTER TWENTY-FOURTH Street, she glanced down at old clothes, worn shoes, and broken small appliances set out on flattened cartons.

The merchandise came from mountains of trash bags set out on the sidewalks on pickup days. Homeless people had become entrepreneurs.

Daisy had once found a signed lithograph by Raphael Soyer on a curb, and never forgot how it shone beside the trash in the moonlight.

She followed Mr. Black across Twenty-Third Street.

She followed him across Twenty-Second Street, cradling the jar in the crook of her arm.

They crossed Twenty-First and passed a coffee shop.

The wine jar was heavy. By Sixteenth Street, she felt as if she were carrying a bowling ball. Her hand was sweaty.

She hooked the handles on her index finger and slung the bag over her shoulder.

They were still on the east side of Sixth Avenue, quickly crossing the little streets below Fourth Street.

At Houston Street, Mr. Black turned east.

Daisy was bound to see someone she knew.

At the corner of Thompson, Mr. Black crossed on just one light. Daisy looked left. Suddenly, she was lifted in the air.

"Put me down! Put me down!" she cried, feeling for her glasses in her pocket.

"Summerfall Winterspring!" her old boyfriend Joe De Leo said.

An Italian woman seated outside her shop on a wooden chair watched cynically.

Daisy said, "I'm tailing someone. See that guy in the Hawaiian shirt? I have to find out where he lives."

Mr. Black turned the corner.

"Hurry, Joe!"

At Prince and Thompson, Daisy stopped beside a grocery store, out of breath.

She saw Mr. Black enter a building.

Joe came back. "Want me to go in?"

As a contractor, he had renovated several small buildings in the area.

"My Aunt Florence lives there."

Oh, no. The murdered woman, Florence Vito, was his aunt?

"Florence Fanuzzi."

"Hoh." Daisy let out her breath and looked across the street at the bakery.

"What's that still doing there?" she asked. "I bought a postcard of that bakery once and thought I was so lucky to get it.

"It's in a time warp," she went on, forgetting about Mr. Black for the moment. "It looks like a super-realist sculpture. Does someone pay to keep it there? What a great art form! There's no art anymore."

"Watch it, Summerfall. You haven't seen my funnels yet."

She fluffed her hair.

Joe tried some keys and opened the door.

Daisy patted his once familiar back.

The mailboxes weren't in the vestibule as she remembered from the early sixties. Inside a second door, the mailboxes were sprayed gold, and the first name, Dawn Dishwashing, made her heart sink.

But when Joe gave her a pen and paper and she started copying, she saw real names.

And one of the names was J. Black.

AT A restaurant on Sullivan Street, the maître d', or the owner or a hit man, greeted Joe.

"This lady is the love of my life," Joe said. "She don't eat no meat, *capisce? Vegetale solamente.*"

"So," he said. "My funnels. You know who bought one? Henry Taig. He's got two of your pieces."

Daisy laughed. "No, he does not! He's a New York City detective."

"You're thinking of his son. I'm talking about the old man. He and his wife threw a party last Wednesday."

"For your funnel?"

"Yeah." Joe's small black eyes gleamed. "There I am, with you and Stella."

MONDAY

Daisy was smiling as she came home from Joe's loft. It had been good to be with someone.

She actually loved his new work, six-foot aluminum funnels. The two that were completed in his loft stood upside down on their cones. They looked like stoves reflecting the room, the tube being the chimney, or stack.

Aluminum was ghastly material to work with snips and crimpers, and his workmanship was beautiful.

"It isn't too bad if you've done custom ductwork," he said.

"I know you and your father made stovepipes and pie plates."

"You remember!"

"If good honest labor were still respected," Daisy thought, "Joe wouldn't have thought of being an artist."

BACK HOME, Daisy looked up the Sixes in the Manhattan phone book.

"Come for tennis!" cried Bunny.

"I can't. I want to read you a list of names, to see if you know one of them.

"J. Black." She held her breath.

"Nope."

"C. Chen."

"No."

"A. Hall."

"Cousin Arthur?"

Daisy had to laugh. "These names are from a tenement on Prince Street!"

"We'll get him to come and play tennis with you. He collects Gaudy Dutch. Maybe you can get him to stop dyeing his hair."

"FAMOUS ATTICS."

"Hi. You know me from the flea market. Do you still have that big set of Fiestaware? Did it belong to Mrs. James Six the Third?"

"I can't tell you that."

"She wants it back."

"She'll have to pay three hundred bucks."

"WHAT CAN I do for you?" asked Taig.

"Do you know who shot Florence Vito?"

"No. Not yet."

"The Sixes didn't have Gaudy Dutch," Daisy said, moving on. "I told you there was a big set of Fiestaware at the flea market. It was theirs. She sold it!"

"I thought it was something like that."

"You knew she was crazy?"

He had known Bunny Six all his life.

She was often away at McLean's fighting the schizophrenia that plagued her distinguished family.

He had last seen her two weeks ago, limping in high heels she said came from the thrift shop, at the party for his father's latest sculptor, Joe De Leo.

The guest of honor, a big homely guy with small dark eyes, had spent the evening in a clearing with his sheet metal funnel.

"It's Henry's method of bamboo control," Taig heard his mother say.

"I FOUND the Sixes' china and solved a murder."

"That's terrific. I wish I had time to talk," Daphne said. "I just came home to change. We're going to a lawn party."

"Daphne, do you know Henry Taig? Henry Taig Sr.?"

"They own two of your sculptures. You know their son is a New York City cop. He's about ten years younger than we are. I bet you'd like him!"

"It's okay."

"Are you seeing someone?"

"I saw Joe De Leo."

"He's becoming quite well known."

"Did you see his funnels? The Taigs bought one."

"I'm not surprised."

"What does Alan think of them?"

"You know Alan. Let me go. I don't know what to wear."

DAISY THOUGHT that wrapping things up was worth a trip up to Horsefly. She arrived at the Sixes' home in a taxi from the train station.

"I forgot I sold them," Bunny told her. "Those dishes had cost us fifteen dollars at the thrift shop. James wants to keep the profit."

The gardener raised cold blue eyes. "Nevah give away money."

So the man without socks wasn't Bunny's gardener, and Daisy doubted James Six was a descendent of Rembrandt's melancholy friend.

IT WAS only a two-mile walk into town and Daisy swung along, looking forward to telling Taig that Bunny's cousin Arthur Hall had killed Florence Vito.

How many china-crazed gunmen could there be in Manhattan? She actually didn't want to think about that. She'd let Taig take it from here.

At the Baker's Cafe across the street from the station, Daisy bought coffee and a raisin scone to go.

Back at the station, she struck up a conversation with an interesting-looking man who was cleaning the platform.

"I'm sorry," he said. "I have to go now."

The sky turned pink. An hour went by before more people came.

At last she heard the train's harmonic whistle and saw its light.

The Little Notebook

1991

SATURDAY

"Did anyone call 911?" she asked the big man to her left.

Daisy was still two blocks from the flea market when she saw a small group of people concerned about a sick derelict.

As she looked at the pay phones across Twenty-Fourth Street, she heard sirens.

They got louder and an ambulance pulled up.

By the time they put the man on a stretcher, everyone knew he was dead.

No chalk mark was traced around his body. No yellow tape preserved the scene.

A bottle lay on the sidewalk.

"They should take that," Daisy said to the big man standing next to her.

"He wass an attick."

"They still should take it!"

Standing over the liquor bottle, she tried to convey to passing strangers that she was waiting for a friend near the topless bar on the corner.

At last, people moved on. She took a tissue from her pocket, picked up the bottle, and carried it around the corner and down to the deli and asked for a plastic bag.

DAISY WAS talking to a dealer named Moe when she saw a Chinese vase carved with peonies and covered by a thick white celadon glaze.

She went over to it, picked it up in both hands, and turned it over. It was heavy.

Moe said, "That's from the thirties."

If he thought it was Art Deco, she knew he'd charge a lot.

"How much is it?"

"Fifty."

"I'll give you forty."

A fall breeze blew faded blond wisps from her ponytail as she studied it through the lower part of her glasses.

"I can't do that."

The surface was scarred by millions of tiny bubbles in the greenish-white glaze. When she looked inside it, holding it toward the sun, she saw orange translucence.

The carving, the glaze, the shape, and the orange light all testified that it had been made in China during the Sung dynasty.

She set it down, playing it cool. Daisy edged between his tables to see what else he had brought.

She once bought a blue-and-white jar from him. From *Sotheby's Concise Encyclopedia of Porcelain* she learned that the jar was Annamese. Made in the northern region of Vietnam in the sixteenth century, it was "neither translucent nor did it 'ring' like Chinese porcelain."

"Thirties," she muttered, extracting something blue and white, the bottom half of an old cardboard box.

In it were a seashell—a volute; and a clump of paper—a little notebook. Only the back of the pink-spotted red paper cover remained.

She read,

> So dainty her dance
> on a pink petal
> I could not tell her
> she was make-believe.

She heard, "You have the right to remain silent. Anything you say can and will be used against you in a court of law. You have the right to have an attorney present."

It sounded like a poem, too, and she looked up and saw four uniformed police officers and Detective Taig.

The officer who read Moe his rights pocketed the card and handcuffed him.

"I wanted this box," Daisy said.

"Take it," Moe told her.

"Why are you arresting him?" she cried.

"I'll talk to you in a minute," Taig said, and she caught a look of hope in Moe's bleary eyes.

His hands were cuffed in front. The crowd around the booth was enlarging.

The market manager said, "We'll pack your things for you, Moe."

"Alleged stolen property," Taig said, taking the white Chinese vase.

"Moe didn't steal that," Daisy cried. "He buys his things upstate!"

"I bought it here."

His face was purple. His gray hair lay in wet bangs on his forehead.

He, too, was around fifty, and he looked like he might have a heart attack.

"Reportedly Sung dynasty," said Taig.

"Reported by whom?"

"Insurance company."

"Moe said it's from the thirties!"

No one heard Daisy.

They were going out the exit to the blue-and-white police cars double-parked at the curb.

"Tell them who you bought it from," she called to Moe.

"I don't know."

She watched him being inserted into one of the cars, then she opened her handbag and put in the box.

As the cars drove away, she returned to Moe's booth.

"I wonder who sold him the vase," she said to the market manager.

"A derelict."

"What did he look like? This isn't right."

"I didn't see anything."

She soon made her way to the street through a new group of arrivals.

"Pay at the gate," a market employee called, as though nothing had happened.

BACK HOME, she set the plastic bag with the bottle by her door and called Taig.

"I have a liquor bottle that was lying near the derelict who died on the corner of Twenty-Fourth Street. I don't think the police were at all careful. It smells funny. It was lying right next to him!"

"What do you mean it smells funny? Did you ever smell a derelict or the things they drink?"

"Did you know the market manager saw Moe buy a vase from a derelict?"

"So?"

"So Moe's still locked up? You won't test the bottle? No interest? Who proved that James Lorimer was a killer—"

"Not proved, he left town."

"And gave you the name of Florence Vito's killer—"

"Arthur Hall also left town."

"Can't you look into it?"

"Look," Taig said. "I'm sorry, I really am, but there's no chain of evidence with that bottle. Even if your pillar of society was poisoned, it's worthless."

Fuming, Daisy rode down in the elevator to the street and almost threw the bottle, plastic bag and all, in a trash can. Instead, she walked over to Riverside Park. The dogs always cheered her up.

One man's Scottish terrier screamed and bounded at great speed to greet a friend. The calm owner looked at Daisy and said, "Scotties always go in like the Marines."

Still smiling back in her apartment, Daisy took out the notebook Moe gave her.

> I will be a poet
> and keep in my notebook
> the sound of spring leaves
> flattered by a breeze.

She turned the page.

> Shadows are sudden in winter
> Gray falling on gray grows black
> like a kind hand on my head
> when I stand long at the window.

Facing it:

> Oh, I'm a weed
> of different breed
> a mustard seed
> in tight glass bead.

She turned another page.

> A tiny brown wren
> sat snug in my hand
> and I stroked him
> with careful forefinger.

Madness
threw her book down,
lay smiling
in the sun.

How is it
when nighttime comes
and the flower
folds to sleep?

The little notebook was a fragile relic of an unknown poet. The seashell with it in the box was a *Voluta musica*. It had black markings that resembled music.

SUNDAY

Early that morning, Daisy arranged the *Voluta musica* beside her *Voluta lyrica*, a small brown shell, somewhat rare and expensive. They looked great together on a windowsill.

Her phone rang.

Daphne said, "My hair colorist retired, and the new one made it too red!"

"She must be good, or they wouldn't have hired her."

"It's too red."

"My favorite dealer was arrested for stealing a vase."

"Don't solve another crime!"

"I wanted the vase. I knew it was Sung because it looked like soap or lard."

"You said you were carving porcelain clay."

"That's why I wanted it," Daisy lied.

"Don't forget our party Sunday."

"I won't." Daisy produced a fake cough.

"You're coming even if you come in an ambulance. Do you have something to wear?"

Daisy changed the subject.

"The dealer who was arrested gave me a book of manuscript poems. I want to read you some. I think they're good. They inspired me
to put china words together."

> Plymouth,
> Davenport,
> Longport.
> Pickle Leaf,
> Pickle Dish,
> Pickle Cup.

"I like it," Daphne said.

> Pepper pots,
> Cup plates,
> Come to me
> And bring your mates.

Daphne laughed.

Daisy opened the little notebook at random, and read aloud:

> He and I like
> electric light
> on nighttime trees.

What a disappointment! The poems couldn't be all that old. She
read from the opposite page:

> I took a rose
> and pressed it.
> A dead flower,
> I possess it.

"I like yours better," Daphne said.

A FURNITURE dealer was set up in Moe's Sunday spot at the south-east corner.

Daisy asked the dealers across the aisle if they had seen him. "Maybe he's at the street fair," they said.

On this brilliantly sunny fall day there were fewer dealers than usual. Daisy walked up Sixth Avenue to the street fair but there was nothing there she wanted.

TUESDAY

There was an absence of light in Daisy's apartment which meant a dark day outside. From the window over her kitchen sink, she could see the street. Rain was coming down.

She could probably afford a better apartment with more space and light but higher rent would mean the pressure to make money every year and that would end her freedom.

She opened her china cabinet and took out a square green dish she had bought at a junk shop. A dragon was impressed in the center.

Her phone rang. "Is this Daisy Summerfield?"

"Yes."

"My name is Jane Hammond. I'm a reporter for *The New York Times*."

"Hi."

"I've been assigned to cover the Kodaly Gallery's 75th-anniversary party."

"That's great."

"I'd like to get firsthand accounts from some of the artists."

"Good idea."

"Would you be willing to talk to me?"

Daisy's work was her life, at least it always had been, and Alan Kodaly was of the utmost importance to her work.

"Sure."

"Is this a good time?"

Daisy sat holding the square green dish. The dragon was traveling the sky searching for a flaming pearl.

"Same here," Daisy thought.

The four corners of his sky were deep scratched pools of glaze made iridescent by old age. It was true of the sky through which she would be traveling.

"You know about Philip Kodaly coming from Hungary and working for Ben Rubenstein?" Daisy asked.

"Oh, yes. I've read everything in our files and spoken to Alan Kodaly. What can you tell me about showing at the Kodaly for the past twenty-five years?"

"Thirty, at least."

"How did you first meet?"

Alan's father, Philip Kodaly, said nothing as Daisy unpacked her soft straw Mexican bag. It was Alan who asked Daisy to show her work with them, but his father had the final say.

Being young and living in a hotel, she had wrapped her clay figures in toilet paper.

José de Creeft was at the gallery that day, and he called Daisy an artist. Only an artist knows another artist and Philip Kodaly was guided by that.

"You've been with the Kodaly a long time," Jane said.

"You make art for yourself, but when someone believes in your work, you do it for him, too. You picture him when you work. You feel less lonely. It makes you feel welcome—that your work will be welcome."

"Did Philip Kodaly encourage your work?"

"Yes, but he was encouraging his son. Alan had just been made a director. My work was his work."

"I've never heard it described that way before."

"An artist's career is formed by a gallery."

Jane Hammond's keys were clicking and Daisy waited for her to catch up.

"There are many famous artists in the Kodaly Gallery stable."

"Right."

"Did you find that daunting?"

"No. If I could go back to what I was saying?"

"Please."

"Artists work alone. They can't meet the public. The gallery creates an artist's persona and presents it to the public. It's the same kind of work as an artist's. An artist sees something on another plane and tries to make it intelligible."

"Thank you. You've given me insight into what a gallery means to an artist."

"Oh, and of course, we need them to sell our work. You can't grow if you have all your work around you."

She had given the Witness sculpture back to Alan once she retrieved it from the police.

SATURDAY

Another furniture dealer was set up in Moe's Saturday spot. Determined to buy something, Daisy entered a booth that sold salt and pepper shakers.

A blue heron was standing on one leg beside cattails on a yellow pepper pot.

The reverse was a blue dragonfly.

She stared at it in disbelief.

A small old woman said, "That's five dollars."

She was too amazed to open her bag.

"I have to get five because it's Chinese and it's old. I don't have the mate for it. I keep it here, hoping someone who has the mate will see it. Maybe you can find the mate to it."

Daisy opened her bag and took out five dollars.

"I'll make it four because I don't have the mate. If I had the mate, I'd have to charge ten. This is a Chinese salt shaker. It's very old."

"I like it," Daisy said. "I love the colors. There's a little black mixed with the blue."

"I can see you're a very interesting and original person," the old woman said, dropping the antique English pepper pot into a small brown sack.

SUNDAY

Somehow the whole day went by, and Daisy just had time for a shower.

She put on white socks, stepped into low-heeled black pumps from Agnès B., and took a pink, blue, cherry-red, and white silk kimono out of her closet.

It was an antique ikat weave, very pretty and festive, but she had never tried it on. She now realized that she had to wear it with jeans and a T-shirt.

She pulled back her hair and fastened it with her plastic barrette.

She looked into her mirror at her small oval face, straight nose, and brown eyes behind steel-rimmed glasses.

She was late. Sliding a twenty-dollar bill into one of her front jeans pockets, she locked her door, put her keys in the other pocket, rode downstairs, and took a cab through the park.

CAMERAS FLASHED as Alan kissed her and said, "I liked your quote in the *Times*."

Lulu King said, "May I?" and took Daisy's small face in her hands and kissed her.

Daisy went to a buffet table. She was vegetarian and she tried to be vegan. When she went to openings, she stuffed herself with fresh vegetables.

Starving artists were not invited to these parties, so much food was wasted.

At the buffet, she met a man named Chris.

". . . sculpture," she heard him say above the loud music and chatter.

She nodded, smiling.

He was a writer, and Daisy was glad to hear that. He would probably be near the buffet table all evening.

One Christmas, an art critic took Daisy to a party at his agent's
office.

The agent said the piece on Daisy's work was the best in the critic's
new book.

He introduced her to his authors and their spouses.

When she spoke about their books, their hungry eyes begged her
to say more.

Others looked on eagerly.

She was a reader!

The only food at that party was an enormous wheel of cheese that
might have represented the earth in a low-budget disaster movie.

Odd-shaped pieces were constantly being cut off and wolfed down
until crumbs remained.

These were put together and eaten by a shaggy writer who never
left the cheese's side.

The guests patted their stomachs when saying good night, then
took the elevator down to the silent lobby and went out to the dark and
snowy midtown street.

IN THE most crowded part of the room, a spotlight hit Daisy's black
wooden ark on its case-hardened limestone block. It was made of wood
and painted black, on loan from the Seattle Museum.

Nearer by, she saw Jack Katz in his rust-colored corduroy jacket,
his blue eyes full of fun.

"Did you see your sculpture?" Katz asked.

"Yes."

He described its beauty to her.

His wall sculptures of twigs, string, and bits of paper were complex
and beautiful.

He was now painting them industrial colors: orange and green, and
white and black.

She wanted one, but they were fragile dust traps. Secretly, Alan said the work made him think of guano, his expressive dark eyes shining with humor.

The conversation turned to Katz's new accountant who told him he spent too much money on books.

"I hate wasting my time on earth doing stupid things like keeping a ledger," Daisy said. "Why are taxes so complicated? Why do movie companies get tax breaks from cities and states? So politicians can meet movie stars. The rest of us get a higher tax bill. Why is that right?"

"It's artists who make terrible neighborhoods trendy," Jack said.

"And then we get kicked out!" Daisy cried. "And if the government could force the Cherokee to leave Georgia, why can't the government force everyone out of Florida? Leave it to the pelicans and panthers and Seminoles. Artists should clean up the country. The galleries could document our work."

"You know," Jack said, "Barnett Newman ran for mayor of New York on the Artists' ticket."

"I didn't know that!" Daisy cried. "There's a photo of Barnett Newman, Betty Parsons, and Jackson Pollock in front of an elevator. I thought it was an elevator, but it was one of Newman's paintings!"

"Did you go to the flea market today?" he asked.

She said, laughing, "I collect old china. I like to take it home and wash it."

"You need to talk to someone here!" Katz looked around. "She owned an incredibly valuable vase until it was stolen and the doofus tried at sell it, right out in the open, at the flea market! Can you believe it? I mean talk about geniuses, right?"

Katz finally pointed out the owner of the vase, a strawberry blond across the room. She was wearing a short strapless black-velvet dress— and wearing it well.

She was with a man who seemed familiar to Daisy.

"I'd love to talk to her," Daisy said.

With Katz at her side, Daisy made it over to them.

"Hi," she said to both of them. "I'm Daisy Summerfield."

"I'm a fan," said the man.

"Thanks!"

"I love your kimono."

"Who are you?" Daisy asked him.

"Osmond Fox."

"I knew I knew you from somewhere!"

His shop was uptown from James Rose Antique China on Madison Avenue. Daisy sometimes went in and looked around.

"Ask for me next time please!" he said.

He introduced her to the strawberry blond, Paige Williams.

"Tell me about the vase at the flea market," Daisy said. "How did it get stolen?"

Paige's apartment in Chelsea was burglarized and the thief made off with a Sung vase Paige had only just purchased from Osmond Fox.

"Imagine! Of course, I was devastated," Paige said dramatically, as if on a witness stand. "I love having beautiful things and Osmond told me it was a good investment."

Osmond smiled at Paige sympathetically. "I understand your pain."

"The insurance company sent out an alert and New York's Bravest swooped down on the crook," Paige said.

"New York's Finest, you mean," Daisy corrected her. "New York's Bravest is the motto of the fire department."

Paige gave Daisy a look she hoped was withering.

"Quite," she said with icy dismissiveness.

"Quite," Daisy mimicked back.

Fox was oblivious. Katz was enjoying it immensely.

"Daisy," he said. "Let's go see Daphne! Nice chatting with you all."

DAISY SAW an empty cab coming but didn't take it.

"I'll walk up to Eighty-Sixth and take the bus," she thought, hearing her little heels tap romantically.

She was surprised to see so many people on the street when she would normally be in bed.

Daisy felt fresh and neat, not drained and soiled as usual after a social event.

As the bus went through Central Park and turned down Columbus Avenue, the word acetone entered her mind.

The bus turned right. After two more avenue blocks, Daisy stepped down to Broadway.

MONDAY

S he woke up the next morning wondering why she was thinking of acetone.

Daisy trusted her subconscious.

She didn't judge her work. She wondered, "Who are you? What are you saying? How can I help you?"

Sometimes she had to work fast, changing tools blindly, using them instinctively. She said the hardest part of being an artist was looking at your work and trying to understand it.

Acetone was one of the solvents she'd researched to remove paint from the Elers cup. In books such as *Artist Beware* and *The Artist's Complete Health and Safety Guide*, she was horrified that many common artist materials were poison.

"Do not use. Cancer agent."

"The skin will absorb resulting in severe liver damage."

"Lethal when combined with alcohol."

"THE PARTY was great!" Daisy told Daphne over the phone.

"So glad you enjoyed it! It really was a wonderful event."

"Daphne, do you know a woman named Paige Williams?"

"I went to college with her."

"You aren't friends with her!"

"We're friendly."

"Did you invite her?"

"No, but I'm glad she came. She's a painter."

"Is she any good?"

"I don't know."

"Does she have a gallery?"

"No."

"I'd like to see her work."

"She'll be thrilled!"

"Make a date, but don't tell her I'm coming."

"Why?"

"She'd be nervous."

DAISY THOUGHT she understood it now.

She called Taig.

"I used to think finding an object could change my life," she told him. "You're happy before you buy something and your money is still your own. You pay for it and leave the shop—a star. Then you get home and unwrap it.

"You look in the mirror, and your eyes look scared. You have less money. Are you listening?"

"Yes."

"So let me tell you what I think happened. Someone buys a Sung vase she really can't afford. She can't take it back without losing prestige, so she starts thinking about the insurance money.

"She gives the vase to a derelict and tells him to sell it at the flea market. Probably tells him he can keep the money and gives him a bottle as a reward. Only she poisoned the alcohol to cover her tracks. And then she calls the insurance company, making up a robbery. Then you arrest poor Moe."

There was a pause.

"You realize that's not what happened," Taig said. "Crime is really mostly scared or angry people doing something dumb."

"You mean the kinds of crime you solve!"

Taig laughed. "The police are an arm of the law. We don't work creatively. Maybe you should just irritate the owner of the vase and get her to leave town."

WEDNESDAY

It felt odd to be in Chelsea on a weekday.

Paige lived in a small, lifeless building near Twenty-Sixth Street and Eighth Avenue.

A small self-service elevator took them up.

Paige opened the door wearing a black-and-gold kimono and kissed Daphne.

"I brought Daisy Summerfield," Daphne said, and Daisy entered with them.

Daisy saw a shawl draped over a bamboo table and thought the Sung vase might have stood there.

She peered down, looking for a round indent mark.

Above the tweed sofa hung two dingy abstracts. "Are those yours?" she asked.

"Yes." Paige stood back to admire them. "They're about paint."

"About wrecking it," thought Daisy.

Poor little tubes, three to a box at the art store. A hand comes down . . .

"It's Paige!" they scream.

"You're so prolific!" Daphne exclaimed, as they entered Paige's studio.

"I'm very driven." She turned some canvases around.

"You're like Cézanne," Daisy said. "His walls were this color."

Cézanne's walls had looked gray when she stood in his modern studio in the hills outside Aix-en-Provence but were green on the postcard she bought there.

On the way back to the living room, Daphne hissed, "Are you crazy?"

Paige served them drinks.

Daisy set hers down.

Daisy imagined her last words, with her last poisoned breath, ending up as a *Post* headline, "LET MOE GO!"

Daisy reached toward a dish, saying in an English accent, "I will chawnce a nut. This reminds me of a time my family was watching

Masterpiece Theatre. We knew the chocolates were poisoned, so when the killer said, 'Have a delicious bonbon,' I screamed, 'NO!'

"Did I ever tell you that?" Daisy asked Daphne. "That was a big joke in our family."

"Have a delicious bonbon!"

"This is a great apartment," Daphne said.

Daisy took a plastic bag from her pocket, put her hand inside it, picked up her drink, and closed the bag over it, saying, "Maybe I'll drink this later."

Daisy shrugged. "You introduce two old friends to each other. They're jealous and behave badly."

She got up.

"We have to go."

Daisy turned the lock, opened the door, motioned to Daphne, and pushed her out.

"What's wrong with you?" Daphne cried.

The elevator came and they rode down.

As they got out, Daisy said, "She uses acetone and she has a copy of *Artist Beware!*"

They opened the door and were back on Twenty-Sixth Street. Daisy hailed a cab.

The driver waited to hear their destination.

Daisy leaned forward. "Eighty-Third and Park."

The cab turned north, hurling them into Daisy's corner.

She took something from her pocket.

The taxi stopped at a light and Daphne saw it was one of Daisy's mallets.

"Why did you bring one of your mallets?"

The cab shot forward and their heads hit the ceiling as a tire went into a pothole.

"I hope this glass is okay," Daisy said.

"WE JUST passed my street."

Daisy risked leaning forward and told the driver, "We'll get out here."

She handed him money and they crossed Park Avenue and walked back downtown.

There were tall broad buildings pierced with yellow light as far as the eye could see.

"It's so good to see you!" Daphne's doorman greeted Daisy.

The wizened old elevator man took them up to the Kodalys' vestibule.

"Thanks, Rodney."

"Thanks," echoed Daisy.

Alan kissed them. "Were you girls drinking?"

"I must reek!"

Daisy went to the downstairs bathroom.

"She's insane," Daisy heard as she bent over the sink and examined the liquor glass.

"Do you have baggies?" she asked Alan.

She followed him to the kitchen, saying, "I saw a wino die a horrible death. Are you sure I don't smell?"

"At least," Daisy thought, "I have Paige's fingerprints on the glass." Daisy would bet anything that they were also on the derelict's bottle.

DAISY CAME into the living room and sank down on the white sofa to the left of the fireplace.

This room contained Daisy's first woodcarving, *The Niece of Mademoiselle Pogany.*

She'd had it made into a lamp with a pink silk shade and given it to Daphne and Alan.

The only other art was a black painting by Ad Reinhardt over the mantel.

When Daisy saw her old sculpture, she remembered crawling on the floor of her room at the Buxton Hotel for Women, picking up wood chips.

Daphne had taken Alan to see her work in one of the cozy parlors on the mezzanine.

The pink silk shade glowed with memories as the three friends sat talking.

THURSDAY

L ast night had been like old times.

Daisy thought of a journal she'd kept in those days, and found it in her closet.

> *I went to the tool shop I had often passed on Sixth Avenue below 13th St.*
>
> *The elderly man who waited on me made me describe my work and the tools I already owned.*
>
> *He said that was all I needed and refused to sell me anything until I could bring my tools to him for inspection.*
>
> *He thought they might need to be sharpened, but reminded me that woodcutting is a slow and beautiful process that must not be rushed.*
>
> *I still think I could use a bigger chisel, but will wait and see.*

She had also copied out parts of poems by Michelangelo, translated by Joseph Tusiani. She had internalized them.

She thought that in the great scheme of things, Michelangelo had carved and painted in order to have subject matter for poetry, his far greater work.

> *The greatest artist has no single concept*
> *Which a rough marble block does not contain*
> *Already in its core*
>
> *He who made all created first each part*
> *Then chose the one most beautiful and bright*
> *To show therein the limit of his might*
> *And the divine achievement of his art*
>
> *With so much servitude, with so much anguish,*
> *And with false concepts periling my soul,*
> *Sculpt I must here on earth, bright things of heaven.*

She flipped to the back of the journal. She had ended it by writing:

I love writing because you can keep it for a long time and change a word or line or title.

    There is no reason to show it prematurely.

    Sculptures are not comfortable things to have around, so if you are lucky you exhibit your work and sell it, not realizing that what you should fear most is success.

IT WAS another beautiful fall day and Daisy decided to walk to the museum.

The bus was coming as she got to Amsterdam, so she counted her change and climbed aboard.

She went back across Fifth Avenue and along the paving stones to the steps. Entering the Great Hall, she stood in line at an admissions booth and paid a dime instead of the suggested six dollars.

Then she walked up to the mezzanine and started down the corridor, looking at Chinese ceramics.

She came to the Koreans. They were true artists, creating with no regard for perfection.

She saw the painted cranes she loved, and the high-shouldered and curved Maebyong vases.

Returning, she stopped to look at a Kwan Yin. The label had the new pinyin spelling, "Guanyin."

A grayish-white jarlet painted in underglaze blue looked like her square green dish. The label said "Ming dynasty."

An impressed green dragon on a white porcelain dish also was Ming dynasty.

Ming blue-and-white only became popular after it was copied by the Japanese, the Dutch, and the English. Now Staffordshire blue-and-white is the most loved china in the world, Daisy had read.

Dragons chasing flaming pearls, Michelangelo's "Sculpt I must."

"We're all here," she thought, "chasing bright things of heaven."

SATURDAY

At the flea market, she got a tiny green plastic dog charm. Then she stopped at a booth where the dealers were a mess. Everything they had was broken and useless, but she had bought good things from the creased-and-swarthy toothless couple before.

She saw a blue-and-white teapot printed with seashells, her favorite motif.

Inside she found the handle and two dried-out dusty old tubes of paint. The spout was chipped in an attractive way.

The woman came over to her and said, "I gotta get fifty for the teapot."

"Do you have the lid?"

"Not if you don't see it."

Daisy put it back.

"Give me forty.

"I collect china," she said, caressing Daisy's bills. "We're bringing more next week."

BATHED IN blue light from the TV, Daisy was watching *The Doubleday Game.*

The seashell-motif teapot, clean and mended, stood on a nearby sculpture stand, ready to be looked at during commercials. Meanwhile, on TV, author Ed Yowder was frantically putting copies of his new book in second-floor sections where he thought they would sell.

His score was minus fifty points.

The first-floor manager, Tom White, was kind to authors. He allowed Ed one point for each book he placed there, leaving him with minus four points.

After the second break, the author stood next to the host.

"Ed, you didn't win *The Doubleday Game* but the Doubleday Bookstore wants you to choose any book to take home.

"Your fans are waiting for you to autograph books of yours they just bought.

"We sold fifty-one copies of *Stars and Scallions* on the first floor to-night. We hope you won new readers—viewers who weren't aware of your books before. You're a good sport and a great writer. Your books carry the power and beauty of your convictions. We hope you'll write many more."

The author sat down at the table that had been prepared for him, and his fans lined up while, to the tune of the theme song, closing credits came on the screen.

Daisy's phone rang.

"Do you think it's true?" asked Daphne.

"What?"

"That authors rearrange the shelves."

"That's how they got the idea."

"I just wanted to see if you were watching."

SUNDAY

Daisy came home with another plastic charm—a yellow bulldog on a purple cord.

She put it in the poet's box, and opened the notebook and read,

> Down, down he sank
> to the bottom
> of the green lake
> Minnetonka,
> a turtle carved
> from opal rock.

Lake Minnetonka was where she was from!

> Here are the small
> colored bits of my soul.
> Wait, I'll toss them at you
> like confetti!

Daisy had an idea. She would type up the poems and write an introduction to them.

Instead of saying they were by an unknown poet, she would give her a name.

She had a small plastic box of loose tintypes. The images, taken by a multi-lens camera, had been cut apart with tin snips.

Two were of a young woman in a black straw hat who was smiling. She could be the poet.

That was rare, though as Beaumont Newhall said in *The History of Photography*, tintypes were cheap and casual and characteristic of a kind of folk art.

Daisy liked the little ones, three-fourths of an inch by one inch, and under.

She could measure hers and find out from *A Century of Cameras* by Eaton S. Lothrop Jr. if they were taken by the Lancaster, the New Gem, the Nodark, the Operateur, the Quta, or the Wing.

For local background, Daisy also had *Minnetonka Story* by Blanche Nichols Wilson, *Once Upon a Lake* by Thelma Jones, *The Saga of Saga Hill* by Theodore C. Blegen, and *Mileposts on the Prairie: The Story of the Minneapolis & St. Louis Railway*, by Frank P. Donovan Jr.

The lake and the Big Woods had been discovered by white men in 1822. By the late 1800s, it was a summer resort for southerners.

The cardboard box with the little notebook inside might have traveled in a trunk from Minnesota. The contents of the box could be presented as relics of the poet's life.

The seashell, *Voluta musica*, was from the Caribbean. How did it come to the poet?

There was a romance. Daisy auditioned male tintypes.

"I'M GOING to buy a typewriter," she told her favorite elevator man, Modesto. "If someone comes to see me, will you ask him to wait?"

Walking over to Amsterdam, she looked back and saw Paige Williams enter her building.

After a while, she saw her leave.

"You missed your friend," said Modesto.

"She's not my friend! She killed someone!"

When they got to her floor, she asked, "Could you bring her up and stay outside my door?"

She got him her cordless phone.

"If she tries to kill me, call 911!"

They heard the buzzer. "It's the lobby," he said, looking at the panel.

"I'll be quick. I'll try to make her confess to the murder."

He closed the elevator and she went back inside and locked the door.

Her other phone rang.

It was her parents calling from Minnesota.

She said, "I'll call you back."

She heard her doorbell, looked out the peephole at Paige, and called, "Just a minute!"

The elevator was on the same side as her apartment, though luckily not next to it.

She opened the door and Paige entered.

Daisy hoped Modesto was outside. "I'm sorry I was rude to you," she enunciated loudly.

"That's not why I'm going to kill you."

"Kill me?" she projected. "Like you killed the wino?"

Daisy thought she heard the beeps of her phone keypad.

"No, I'm going to push you out the window."

"In murder mysteries," Daisy could hear her own hayseed voice as if on tape, "the murderer confesses *before* killing the amateur detective."

Paige grabbed her arm. "You haven't done any sculpture in years. You're depressed and you're committing suicide."

Paige pulled Daisy across the room toward the window.

"STOP! STOP!" Daisy yelled. Her seashells were on the windowsill.

"Police! Open up!"

"It's open!"

Modesto easily held Paige's arms behind her back. "I called," he told Daisy.

A female officer arrived quickly and read Paige her rights.

"Don't you have cuff links? Lucky I have a cordless," Daisy babbled to the officer.

The first time Daisy saw a woman cop, she had thrown down her dishtowel and run downstairs to congratulate her.

"Haha!" Daisy laughed inanely. "I said 'cuff links.' I meant 'handcuffs.'"

The officer and Modesto were speaking Spanish.

Taig came in looking frantic. He had heard her address on his scanner.

"You okay?" he said.

"Have a delicious bonbon," she said coolly.

She opened her tool chest, got the liquor glass and bottle in their plastic bags, and told the officer to hold them upright.

SATURDAY

"Hi," Moe greeted her.

"Hi."

Looking down, she saw a shallow bowl, a Chinese export saucer from the mid to late 1700s.

A lozenge had a festoon of tiny magenta and red flowers, green leaves, and a magenta ribbon. In the lower center were large airy gold initials.

Above it, two clasped hands were outlined in gold, and above them two *bistre*-and-white doves with red beaks and feet stood facing each other on a rolled-up marriage contract.

The saucer was mended. She showed Moe the rivets.

"Ah, it's broken," he said. "I didn't see that."

"But the way it's fixed is great."

"You know what that is?"

"I just like the staples." Thick and black, they had rusted into the translucent body.

She would have to accept it as a token of his thanks. In fact, she would love it.

"How much is it?"

"Twenty to you."

"You've got to be kidding," she said, her face numb with shock.

But he had given her the box with *Voluta musica* and the poems, so she paid and started to leave.

"Wait," he said. "What did you take from me that day?"

"Half a cardboard box."

"There was something in there."

"Junk!"

"Gimme twelve dollars."

"It was on your dollar table!"

"It shouldn't have been there. You can bring it back next week. You know I'll let you do that. That book of writing—that's what the people want. I'm out here to make money," he called after her.

The Blue Glow

1992

FRIDAY

"**A**lan," Daphne said to her husband, "we never got Daisy a fiftieth birthday present."

"Does she want one?"

"Did I want these?" She closed the clasp on her pearls.

"Do you want to give them to Daisy?" His dark eyes looked worried as he knotted his tie.

"No, I love them!"

"Should we get her pearls?"

On this sweet spring morning, in the beautiful New York light that had impressed Matisse, the thought of casting pearls before swine came and went.

"I was angry when she stopped carving. I thought she was disloyal to you."

Alan stopped collecting the things from his bureau top.

"She never made those porcelain sculptures she talked about."

"I guess they weren't compelling."

"I want to get her something at James Rose."

It had been three years since the flare-up and apology from Rose about the Elers cup. Leon was back at the shop now as well.

"His prices start at two thousand dollars!"

"We get a discount."

"Only twenty percent."

"I could go there after class and see if there's something wonderful."

He kissed her smooth auburn hair and said, "I think it's a great idea. Now, I have to go. There's an early meeting."

As Daphne put in her earrings, she remembered Daisy asking about them, and wondered if she would like diamond earrings.

They had given her a white jade necklace they never saw her wear.

Daphne wanted this gift to bring them closer.

Across town, Daisy Summerfield slouched around her studio apartment.

Turning fifty was publicly humiliating. Fifty-one was marginally better.

She opened a silk-lined box and took out the white jade necklace and put it on.

Her two mahogany sculpture stands were pushed back against the wall, her tool chest locked.

Cracked old china from the flea market stood on all three surfaces.

She went to her bookshelf and stood in front of a granite Witness she had carved. She lifted it and turned it in her hands.

She decided to go to the Sculpture Shop and buy a stone.

She kept on the necklace. Someone there would admire it, and she would say, "The Kodalys gave this to me."

Carving again, in her small apartment, would mean sleeping in dust and stone chips. That was what she missed. And she wanted to call Daphne and say, "Guess what. I'm carving!"

"Hello, Jim," Daphne said as she walked into James Rose Antique China. It was just past ten o'clock.

"Daphne!"

"Hello, Leon. So glad you're back. I came to get a present," she said.

"We're honored," said Mr. Rose.

"It's for our friend Daisy Summerfield."

The two large men shrank.

"We want to get her something special, something that has a mystery," she said.

"I know she likes early-English pottery," Leon told her and chuckled plummily. "Don't we all."

He showed her the glass cabinet filled with bright-colored earthenware teapots. Near it a low vitrine displayed small green and cream objects.

Daphne put her briefcase on the floor. She could see why Daisy liked these things. They were crude yet refined, and combined humor with real artistry.

One teapot had four feet. Another had a dog for a knob. Another teapot was a kneeling camel.

The buzzer sounded and a gray-haired man came in and started to look around.

Leon went over to him.

James Rose opened the glass cabinet and took out a small teapot. He handed it to Daphne, saying, "This is Astbury. Joshua Astbury pretended to be an idiot so the Elerses would hire him. Then he learned their secrets!"

"How much is it?"

He removed the lid.

"Four thousand."

"Do you have something hidden away that she'd be very excited to own?"

She dismissed the Astbury teapot and everything else on display.

"Maybe you're psychic, Daphne. There is something we've been researching."

He put the teapot back.

"It's not as old as Elers or Astbury, but it is eighteenth century."

He led her to the back of the shop and said, "Sit down. I'll bring it to you."

The gray-haired man was looking in one of the cases along the wall near her seat. His clothes were shabby, but that didn't mean a thing. "On the contrary," Daphne thought.

Leon Rose looked unhappy when his father came from the office carrying a pink-and-white *chinoiserie* figure.

The look on Leon's face made Daphne want to buy it.

It wasn't on display: they were researching it. She thought Daisy would love it.

"How much is it?" she asked.

James Rose answered in a very low voice, "If we could prove that it is Gouyn or Saint Cloud . . ."

Daphne smiled, hearing Daisy say "San Clou."

". . . the sky would be the limit. But I think it's much more than you want to spend."

"How much is it?"

He made his voice even lower. "Seventy-five thousand."

"So the dealer's association discount would make, um"—Daphne did the math—"sixty thousand dollars."

Daisy's last sculptures had sold for $200,000.

The gray-haired man left the shop, and Leon sat down with Daphne.

"Alan will think I'm crazy, and I'll come back and get the white teapot."

"This is better than the teapot. If we could authenticate it, it would go to a museum."

"I want a copy of your research."

"Guyon," Leon began. "Gouyn or—"

"But we don't guarantee it!" James Rose returned with a nicely sealed carton. "I would never let it go for that price if we could guarantee it."

"Understood."

He walked her to the front of his shop. "I hope your friend likes it."

"Let's see what Alan says."

Carrying the little carton, she walked down the block.

"Give it to me," the gray-haired man said to her at the corner.

"Daisy's right," she thought. "People who want old china are insane."

"I'm afraid not," she told him.

In his raised hand he held a pistol by the barrel.

"Is he going to threaten to shoot himself?" she wondered.

DAISY ENTERED her apartment and saw the light on her answering machine blinking.

She hadn't made it to the Sculpture Shop. A new idea made her detour.

"No sooner do I buy paints than the calls come rolling in," she thought, pressing Rewind.

Then she carefully opened a stapled bag from New York Central, preserving the receipt.

She reached in the bag and took out a heavy tube of raw umber as the messages played.

"Daisy, Daphne was hurt. She was hurt very badly."

Beep.

"Daisy, Daphne was hurt. She's at Mount Sinai." The voice wasn't recognizable.

Beep.

"Daisy, call me at Mount Sinai. Ask for Daphne's room. I can't see the extension." He was crying, almost hysterical.

Beep.

Alan?

"Daisy, call me at Mount Sinai as soon as you get in. Daphne's hurt."

She put down the tube. Her bag was still on her shoulder. She thought, "This can't be real."

"TAX-EEEE!"

"Mount Sinai Hospital," she told the driver, praying he knew how to go through the park.

"Are you hurt?" he asked.

"No."

If she were bleeding, he would tell her to get out.

"SOMEONE HIT her," Alan said, standing and turning to face Daisy.

"Oh, no!" Tears sprang to her eyes, and she started trembling.

"Some people from Ohio called the ambulance."

"Did they see it?"

"Yes."

"Did they get the license number?"

"It wasn't a car."

"Mugged? Oh, God, please. When will she wake up?"

"They can't say. Stay with her," Alan said, and left the room.

"She must feel safe," Daisy thought. "She thinks she's dreaming. Her protective system is telling her, 'Don't wake up.'"

"Hi, Daphne! You look pretty. We're at Mount Sinai. It's spring and the air is soft."

Once, years ago, when Daisy was just waking up, she saw a blue glow outside her window. She recognized it as someone's spirit wandering in the night but it got the wrong window.

"You come back to us." She stroked Daphne's hand.

"There are buds on all the trees. When you wake up, we can go to the park. Remember the cherry blossoms last year? I can't wait to see them again."

She saw Alan in the doorway.

"Alan's back," Daisy said. To Alan she said, "Tell her where we live and what we do so she can find us."

"Come out here for a minute," Alan said, and introduced her to Detective Mike Angeli.

"Michael Angeli?"

They went to the room at the end of the corridor and sat down.

Mike was short and stocky. He rested his notebook on his raised thigh. Daisy wondered what was in it.

"The people who called the ambulance saw a man take something from your wife," Detective Angeli said.

"Nothing's missing that I know of," Alan said.

"Where did it happen?" asked Daisy.

"The northeast corner of Madison and Eightieth," Angeli said.

"Near James Rose Antique China," Daisy said.

"Any problem there?"

Daisy said "yes" and Alan said "no" simultaneously. Alan looked at Daisy.

"There was an issue," Alan told Angeli, "but that's in the past. Daphne might have gone there, I don't know. She was talking about it."

"Any other issues, present or past?"

"There's a small one at the gallery."

"Your gallery?" Angeli asked.

"Daphne works there, too," Daisy interjected. "What kind of trouble?"

"A European firm wants to buy us."

"What?" cried Daisy.

"You want to sell?" asked Angeli.

"No," he said.

"Would they hurt your wife?"

"No," Alan said, getting up. "I'm going back to her room."

Angeli looked satisfied. Daisy stood and smiled at him.

"How can you care as much as I do?" she thought.

SATURDAY

Detective Angeli spoke to Leon Rose. He described a gray-haired man with shabby clothes who left shortly after Daphne was attacked.

Leon didn't know the man's name but Leon thought he'd seen him at the Twenty-Sixth Street flea market.

DAPHNE'S CONDITION hadn't changed by Saturday night.

There was no sign of internal bleeding. The CT and MRI looked good. Vital signs were good.

"I'll call you if there's any change," Alan told Daisy.

SUNDAY

Detective Angeli canvassed the flea market with a police sketch Leon helped them create.

Unfortunately, the description, "gray haired with shabby clothes," fit nearly every male dealer there, and so did the sketch.

DAPHNE'S ROOM was filled with flowers.

There were waves of daffodils, "architectural" tulips, and Monet irises.

Magnolia, forsythia, and dogwood branches leaned against clear glass walls, like Van Goghs.

A plain glass tumbler of pansies was a quote from a Matisse at the Met.

Daisy loved that. She'd brought a clean old Higgins ink bottle holding a tiny bunch of violets.

"You should see your flowers," she told Daphne. "Guess what! A young man at New York Central told me I could use wallpaper paste as a ground for painting. I bought watercolor blocks. Canvas never appealed to me. The paste is made from vegetables, and it's reversible. Guess how much it cost? Two dollars!"

DAPHNE'S MIND went down different highways and byways.

One was a curving climbing highway with black-and-white guardrails on the left.

She entered a bathroom with hundreds of stalls. At last she found one she could use.

She was on a top floor of a department store.

To go down she had to use chutes, changing in midair from one to another.

She saw Daisy on the mezzanine and wondered how Daisy had gotten there.

She was packed into a chute with other people who were going on a plane.

She went down one of three roads that led to a river.

She went down another of the roads.

She and some girls were sledding on one of the roads.

They came to a highway.

"How do I sled all the way to the roadhouse," she worried.

She saw Daisy pick up her sled.

"You can carry your sled," Daisy told her.

She heard Daisy talk about painting. "I said you should paint," Daphne thought she said.

"Daisy's painting," she thought she told Alan.

She saw one of her grandmothers and her old dog, Tubby, and her old cats, Gloria and Lulu.

She saw two elms she had known as a child, and the robin who'd teased Tubby in New Jersey.

TUESDAY

On Madison, a beautiful man came toward Daisy, waving at someone behind her. But it was Alan, and he had waved at her.

"Let's get some coffee," Alan said.

Now she would learn which European gallery wanted to buy the Kodaly. Someone there might have hurt Daphne if Alan was refusing to sell.

DAISY LEANED forward with her coffee cup. "Daphne's not just your wife, you know. She's my best friend."

"Why have you been so distant lately?"

"We had dinner on my birthday." She burst out laughing. "That was fun."

He smiled at her.

"I didn't want you to know I'd stopped carving," she said.

"You must know what you're doing. You don't have to make art if you don't want to."

"I thought you cared about my work."

"Daisy, you know I do."

Longing to hear that he cherished her, she found his words cold. Daphne would have known what to say.

"I'll find out who did this," Daisy said.

"No, please, let the police do their work. Just be here for Daphne."

"I'm here all the time! Who wants to buy the gallery?" asked Daisy.

"Wolfsheim."

"Are they after you?"

"No. The director is in town and just made a good offer."

Daisy felt light-headed. "What would you do without the gallery?"

"I'm keeping it."

"Are they angry?"

"No."

"Do you know where they are? Which hotel?"

"I don't know," he said. "They could be anywhere."

He stood up and left without paying.

Daisy threw down money and ran after him.

He was on the next block.

"She'll be fine," Daisy said.

"Are you sure?" he asked shakily. "Because I believe in you."

DAISY CALLED the gallery.

"Melanie?"

"Hi, Daisy!"

Melanie had recently been made a full curator at the Kodaly.

"Can you tell me who's in town from Wolfsheim and where he or she is staying?"

"John de Carville. He's at the Regency."

"Thanks!"

Melanie suddenly sounded worried. "Why do you want to see him?"

"I want to find the person who hurt Daphne. If she's scared to wake up, finding the person could help."

"I'm sure you will."

"Alan doesn't want me to, so keep this between us."

"Why doesn't he?" Melanie said. "Solving crimes is part of your art."

"Really?"

"You carve Witnesses."

"That's brilliant!"

"Maybe I should write your next catalog," Melanie said. "All about your crimes."

WEDNESDAY

Daisy pinned a crumpled pink silk rose to where the sagging neck of her black cardigan made a V.

Delighted with this ensemble, she stepped into low-heeled black pumps from Agnès B. and headed to a small restaurant in the lower East Fifties.

"I'm meeting Mr. de Carville," she told the maître d'.

He took her to a round table covered by a floor-length multicolor paisley-patterned cloth, and pulled out a chair upholstered in a different pattern.

She had to propel the chair over the carpet to a more comfortable position. The polyester cloth tangled with her jeans when she tried to cross her legs.

A waiter came to take her drink order.

She asked for an Evian, no ice.

"Miss Summerfield," said a tall, dark-eyed man, coming toward her.

His blue shirt was so crisp, his tan so brown, his suit so fitted, his cuff links so golden, she nearly stood to greet him.

"This is a great honor," he said. "Have you eaten here before?" He pressed his tie to his chest and sat down. "The food is mahvelous."

"Good, I'm hungry," Daisy said.

He threw back his head and laughed.

There were no prices on the menu. There were three entrées: meat, chicken, and fish. Daisy asked the waiter for a salad.

"All the entrées come with salads."

"I'd like one for lunch."

"The chef's too busy to prepare a salad."

"Then bring me bread and a side salad."

The waiter gave her an ice-filled glass.

"No ice," she reminded him.

"Most of our guests prefer ice."

"I don't!"

John de Carville ordered a scotch. "Americans," he said. "You must spend most of your time in Europe."

"No."

He raised his eyebrows.

"No ice in spring water is just common sense."

"Common sense," he repeated as if he enjoyed the concept. "Was it Epstein who said an artist is not only a dreamer but practical as well? Still, I think that's rare for an artist."

She wondered if he was drunk.

"How can you say that?" she said. "We work with materials. We do things no one has done, and see them through."

"But about practical matters . . ."

"Those are practical matters. If it doesn't work—"

"You blame the assistant."

"I'm talking about real artists!"

"But in money and everyday matters?"

"We may hate it, but we do it," Daisy said.

Rothko's life was tragic because he depended on others.

"I can be cheated," she said, "but not as easily as somebody who doesn't work with her hands."

"And the people who cheat you?"

She drank some warm Evian while he ordered another scotch. "I've solved some crimes."

As they ate, Daisy came to agree with Alan that the Wolfsheim wasn't behind this.

She considered falling in love with John de Carville. She would have a life like Daphne's, only in Europe.

He tasted his third drink.

"You know, you are one of the prizes we would win if we buy the Kodaly," de Carville said.

"Alan isn't selling."

"Maybe we'll convince him."

"Why don't you just open a New York Gallery?"

"Would you leave the Kodaly and come to us?"

"No."

Again he threw back his head and laughed. "You tell it like it is, baby. Dessert?"

The waiter said they had great chocolate cake.

De Carville ordered another scotch, but when Daisy's cake was served, he reached over with his fork and took off the tip and ate it.

Renoir taught his children that whoever takes the tip of a wedge of cheese is a cad.

Daisy had a bite from the back of the cake and put down her fork.

So she had found a cad and that was all.

SATURDAY

The flea market was busy.

Daisy stopped to see a yellow cup. Melted flecks of green and rust were in the yellow glaze.

The cup was light in her hand. Blue was dashed down the front.

As it raced around the rim, it covered three-fourths of the flower and leaf *appliqués* and even the top third of the handle.

She turned it over and saw a brown foot rim.

"How much is this?" she asked.

"There should be a price."

It was six dollars.

"May I have it for five?"

"Sold."

"Daisy!"

She turned and saw Lulu King, the star of the Kuhlman Gallery in SoHo, with John de Carville.

"I heard that Daphne Kodaly was in a coma?" said de Carville.

"She'll be okay," Daisy replied.

"I wish I were in one," Lulu said.

SUNDAY

"Hi, Mom. Happy Mother's Day."

"Thanks. We're just sitting down to breakfast."

"I'm here, too," Mr. Summerfield said. "How's the weather there?"

"Daphne's in a coma."

"How long has she been unconscious?"

"A week. She looks fine, but her brain tissue's swollen and she just sleeps."

"You may think she's just sleeping, but they work with her all the time," her father said.

"They bathe her and brush her teeth and they move her arms and legs so she doesn't lose strength. You may think she's just sleeping, but she's a very busy young woman."

"How do you know all this?"

Her mother said, "*St. Elsewhere.*"

Daisy said, "They take her for CAT scans. So far there's no evidence of bleeding, no subdural hematoma."

"That's good."

"What are they feeding her?" asked her father.

"Glucose."

"Right now, I bet she has a tube in her arm. In a few more weeks it won't be that simple."

"She'll be up before then."

"Did you know she has a catheter inside her leg for urine? There's a bag on the side of the bed."

"That's enough," said Daisy's mother.

"She thinks her friend is just lying there sleeping!"

"Let's hope she'll wake up soon."

"Thanks, Mom."

"How's Alan taking it?"

"He's upset!"

"He could be a widower."

"Dad!"

"I didn't think you and the Kodalys were that close anymore," said her mother.

"We've been friends for thirty-two years!"

"Let's hope you'll be friends for thirty-two more."

"When's your next show?" asked her father.

IN THE third row of booths in the lower half of the antiques lot, Daisy saw some ceramic figures.

A *blanc de chine* Kuan Yin wasn't old, and both hands were missing.

A polychrome Immortal wasn't stamped "China," but it wasn't old, either.

She still felt she would find something there.

There was a seated Oriental figure with Caucasian features and a thin crackled glaze.

She picked it up, turned it over, and found a small white chip in the grayish-white base.

Porcelain is fused, not grainy. If she touched her tongue to it, it would pull at her saliva. She'd need to wash it first, though.

"How much is this?" she asked the gray-haired dealer.

"One fifty. It's Chinese." He had a foreign accent she couldn't place.

"No, it's not!"

"One thirty."

She set it down but didn't leave.

When they were alone, she asked, "What's the lowest price you can take?"

"One twenty."

"I don't have that much."

"It's Chinese," he repeated.

"No, it's not!"

She set it down and picked it up again if someone came too near.

The next time they were alone, she asked, "Can you make it fifty?"

"A hundred."

"I wish I could. I'd pay a hundred dollars to go home."

"You can go home. Go home!"

"I can't! I love this."

"You love it? How much you can pay?"

"Fifty."

"I don't think you're dealer."

"I'm not!"

"If you were dealer, I charge thousands. Rich Madison Avenue dealer, I charge hundred thousands. A dealer say something worth hundred thousand, but that's not what he paid."

"I know!"

"You're okay," he said. "Sometimes customers is no good. They say, 'Give to me for ten, or I drop it.'"

"That's terrible." She noticed his clothes were very worn.

"But not as bad as rich dealers. I bring things here so people can buy. You look poor."

"Do I really look that awful?" Daisy wondered in shock.

"Give me sixty."

SHE TOOK the figure to her kitchen, adjusted the taps to the warmth of summer rain, placed it on a towel, and washed it with soap and a soft toothbrush.

The brush stayed surprisingly clean.

She dried the figure, took it to her desk. She didn't know who the figure was meant to be. One of the eight Immortals? The figure held a scepter.

Then she remembered the Chinaman Teapots and opened *Teapots and Tea* by Frank Tilley. One pot looked very much like hers.

> When this famous and, in fact, almost fabulous Teapot was sold in 1938 at the dispersal of the Wallace Elliot Collection, it was described as probably having for its prototype "a Ting yao piece of the Sung Dynasty."
>
> Honey suggests that the paste and modelling of these Chinaman Teapots may stem from Gouyn or someone previously at St. Cloud
>
> Marks: an incised triangle. Circa 1745. Height: 7".

Daisy measured hers: seven inches.

His pink robe and hat with two long streamers had an impressed pattern. Nothing was on the base, no incised triangle, but an uneven rim of pink showed that the base had been filed.

She thought an incised triangle was the mark for Chelsea, an early manufacturer of English porcelain. The saliva test had been inconclusive.

His face wasn't as strong as the ones in the book. The folds in his robe were neater. The hands looked like the ones in the photos.

It was the hands that compelled her to stay at the booth and get a good price.

His bare arm and hand holding a scepter made her think of ancient sculptures or broken seashells imbedded in sand.

She couldn't find "Gouyn" in her books.

Too late she had learned that scholars keep even the worst books for any crumbs they might contain.

At last she found "Gouyn, Charles" in the index of *The Practical Book of Chinaware*:

> What we believe to be likely is that the factory was established by or, at least, managed by one Charles Gouyn, who is said to have been either a Fleming or a Frenchman, and that his skilled workmen came from France and Germany.

Gouyn's identity and personality are largely conjectural. In his exhaustive book on Chelsea china, William King points out that "the strong resemblance between early Chelsea porcelain and that produced by the French soft paste factories renders it highly possible that Chelsea was started by some refugee from St. Cloud, Chantilly or Mennency, and if this be so, Gouyn may well have been the individual in question."

Her doorbell rang.

Daisy went lightly to the hall and tried to see through the peephole. "Who is it?" she called.

"Detective Angeli."

She let him in and he looked around.

"Are you moving?" he asked. "Or did you just get rid of something?"

"No, I've lived here thirty years. I haven't been working lately."

"What kind of decorating style is this?"

"What do you mean?"

"I thought you were a famous artist. Where's your house? The Hamptons? You should have given me both your addresses."

"Why are you here?" His assumptions were making her edgy.

"Wanted you to see a sketch."

Daisy relaxed. It was sweet really, he wanted to show his artwork.

Angeli handed her a piece of paper and Daisy realized it was a police sketch. The face wasn't familiar.

"Leon Rose helped us with that," Angeli said. "Supposedly, he's a dealer at the flea market, but so far nothing."

"WHAT? Daphne was attacked by a flea market dealer?"

"We don't know that for sure. Leon Rose thinks he remembers seeing him there once. Not a lot to go on. I spoke to that guy with the clipboard, the manager. Nothing."

"I thought I saw you there!"

"Yeah, looks hopeless, but I wanted to check with you. No stone unturned and whatnot. Are you getting new furniture?"

"No."

She was actually starting to like him.

She said, "Sculptors work with negative space. We redefine it. We need space for that. We need light, and we don't want it fragmented on other things."

"Uh-huh," he said.

It was fun having someone to talk to!

"Light is a presence to a sculptor. It's a visitor. We want it to notice one thing.

"Would you like some tea? Come here," she called, going to the kitchen.

She went back to the cupboard and selected a saucer for their used tea bags.

"It's from the flea market," she said.

AFTER SEEING him out, she kept smiling, remembering the way he sat at her table and picked up his mug in both hands and sipped from it.

An artist's life is lonely, and Mike's visit was fun. He was rough but had real sensitivity. It was like pretending to drink tea from acorn cups with the young Jackson Pollock.

MONDAY

Alan looked more worn and miserable every day that passed. Daisy convinced him to go out for coffee.

"You know, Daphne bought you a present at James Rose," Alan said. "It was supposed to be a present from us for your fiftieth birthday."

"When did she buy it? I'm fifty-one."

"It was in the box the people from Ohio saw the mugger take."

"Detective Angeli said he spoke to Leon Rose."

"I brought their description to show you. It was a French or English eighteenth-century pottery figure of Confucius."

He handed her a piece of paper. It read:

"Seated figure, pink hat, pink robe, lotus blossom, and scepter, all underglaze. Black or gray markings on face and beard, also underglaze. Possibly Chantilly, St. Cloud, or Gouyn. Possibly mid-eighteenth century. Height: seven inches."

Should she say, "I just bought that figure!"

"I'm in shock," Daisy said. "I can't believe she got me something at James Rose."

As they drank their coffee, possibilities that she couldn't share with Alan started to come together in her mind.

Either the flea market dealer stole it from Daphne or he bought it from the person who did.

She mentally compared her memory of the dealer's face to Angeli's sketch. She remembered he hated rich Madison Avenue dealers. Maybe he was jealous of Daphne's obvious wealth.

Unless the piece Daisy bought was a copy and there were many of these Confuciuses floating around. "Why did the Roses think it was Confucius?" she wondered.

Alan stood up. They left most of their coffee and went back to the hospital.

SHE CALLED Detective Angeli.

"Yo, Ms. Summerfield."

"Yo, yourself! Can you meet me at the flea market Saturday? It could be very important."

FRIDAY

"You think Alan fell in love with you because of your clothes," Daisy said. "Did you belong to the TAB Book Club when you were in the seventh or eighth grade?

"There was a story in one of the books I bought, *The Date Catcher.*

"A high school girl goes to a department store on an errand. She sees a basket of barrettes on a counter.

"A sign says they're Date Catchers. They're all different colors. You know how sweet plastic colors can be.

"A saleslady picks one and says, 'Try it on.' It looks good on her, and she impulsively buys it.

"She decides to get a Coke at the Sweet Shop where all the kids hang out.

"She's poor and works after school. A popular boy is sitting alone at the counter. He just had a fight with his girlfriend.

"He's never noticed this girl before, but they talk, and he invites her to a dance called the Harvest Festival.

"He pays for her Coke when he leaves.

"She puts up her hand to touch the Date Catcher, just to reassure herself—and it isn't there."

"Ungh."

Did Daphne say that?

Daphne's eyebrows moved. Her eyes opened to tiny slits, and Daisy reached for the bell.

The nurse felt her pulse while looking at her wristwatch.

"She's lightening," she said. "Talk to her some more. She loves hearing your voice."

"Okay," Daisy said, trying not to cry. "I'll tell you another story. I think it's by the same author.

"A boy named Bertie was in the bathroom one morning, when he saw the start of a pimple on his nose.

"He couldn't go to high school with this pimple, so he put a Band-Aid on it.

"It looked like the Band-Aid was covering a pimple, so he added more Band-Aids.

"It still looked like he was covering a pimple, so he found a roll of gauze and wrapped it around his head.

"He wrapped it around his chest and legs.

"When he came down to breakfast, his mother thought he had been in a terrible accident and she almost fainted."

"What's wrong with me?" thought Daisy.

"Hn, hn."

"I thought it was funny. I remembered it all these years!"

Daphne's eyes closed.

"Don't go back to sleep!"

The door opened.

"Daphne's awake," the nurse greeted Alan.

He kissed her hair.

"Darling? Daphne? Are you awake?"

"Hi," Daphne said groggily.

He kissed her and gave her water as Daisy looked away.

"Daisy woke her up," the nurse said. "She was telling her funny stories."

"Funny stories?" Alan asked.

"From books I read in seventh or eighth grade."

"Will you tell them to me?"

"No."

SATURDAY

D aisy paid and entered the flea market. Mike Angeli was right behind her.

"I just walk around and look," she said, picking up a cuckoo clock.

The dealer appeared out of nowhere. "I have to get two-fifty for that."

She put it down.

"You don't like it?" asked Mike. "My grandmother had one like it."

"So did mine. Does it work?" she asked the dealer.

He was helping someone else.

"Must be nice, being a famous sculptor who solves crimes. Alan told me about the detective work you've done."

"There's another detective named Taig—"

"Sure, know him well. He's here today."

Daisy looked around. "Why?"

"I told him what you told me and he volunteered to help. I think he likes you."

"Taig doesn't think I solved any crimes. He thinks I just annoy people until they run away."

They continued walking, Daisy kept looking for the dealer but also for Taig.

"I've been on the force ten years and I never solved a crime," Angeli said.

"You must have!"

"Tell me what cases you solved."

She turned and said, "They all had to do with china."

She saw the gray-haired dealer.

She pointed and yelled, "That's him!"

He was cornered by the fence. Before Angeli could get to him, the dealer pulled a gun.

Something whistled past Daisy's ear.

Dishes in a neighboring booth exploded.

Someone screamed.

Angeli had the dealer on the ground. The dealer was shouting that the real criminals were on Madison Avenue.

Taig arrived with a uniformed cop.

"Police! Everyone okay?"

"Who pays for breakage?" demanded a dealer. "I'm away from my booth fifteen minutes, my table gets shot."

Daisy sank to the ground.

Taig knelt beside her.

"He aimed at me," she sobbed. He put his arm around her and held her to his chest. It felt nice.

"Take him." His deep voice vibrated in her ear, and she looked up and saw Angeli and the cop handcuff the dealer.

"He could have killed a child—or a dog!"

"I'll take over," Angeli said to Taig. "Want to take this guy in?"

"You want to comfort Ms. Summerfield?" Taig asked.

"She and I go back," Angeli said.

"We go back further."

Angeli winked at Daisy.

She once saw a blond detective's long hair flying, his badge bouncing on a chain around his neck. That was how she felt when she was carving. It was why she liked detectives. She could have gone for any one of them.

SUNDAY

Daisy opened her eyes.

"Going to the flea market?" asked Taig.

From the front of her apartment, the kitchen and the bathroom, came the loud reedy voices of birds in the newly leafed trees on Eighty-Sixth Street.

"What do you want for breakfast? I'll go out and get it," he said.

They were embarrassed to get out of bed. She saw her T-shirt and reached for it.

She felt his hand on her back, but she pulled the T-shirt over her head.

Maybe they were both too old to do this gracefully. Maybe they lacked a gift for intimacy.

He swung his legs around, put on his underwear and jeans, and went to the bathroom.

When he came out, she was dressed and it was her turn to use the bathroom.

"Want to get married?"

"No," she called over her shoulder. "Maybe when I'm sixty."

"When's that?"

"Nine years."

"You're fifty-one?" Taig said, astonished.

"How old are you?"

"Forty-two."

"That's a great age. I loved being forty-two."

"DID YOU always want to be an artist?" Taig asked as they sat down at the Argo Diner.

"No! When I was in high school, I wanted to be a movie star."

He nodded.

"My movie-star name was going to be Patricia de la Hunt. I wrote what *Photoplay* would say: 'Cute, pert, little Patty de la Hunt.' Do you think I should write murder mysteries under the name Patricia de la Corpse?"

"No," he laughed, "but you have good instincts. Maybe better than mine."

"I'm glad to hear you think so."

"I always thought your instincts were good. I just worry about you getting hurt."

WALKING WITH Taig, Mr. Flea gave her the thumbs-up. "Is that your boyfriend?" he mouthed.

She smiled and shook her head.

In the next aisle she saw a necklace of silver beads and picked it up. "Let me buy it for you."

"If I want jewelry, I'll buy it," she said, as they walked down the aisle.

MONDAY

Daphne was sitting up, wearing a Viyella robe Daisy had helped her choose.

"See, it still looks good."

"It isn't old."

"Did you learn anything?" Daisy asked, sitting down.

"About what?"

"Life."

"I knew you'd ask that!"

"I think we break off from a whole to test ourselves in a material world," Daisy said. "You didn't see any objects, did you?"

"I didn't see anything," Daphne said, smiling. "I like hearing you talk.

"Detective Angeli and Detective Taig both came to see me."

"Did they tell you I solved the crime?"

"They said you were instrumental as a good citizen in aiding law enforcement."

Daisy hoped they left out the part where she was shot at. Also the part where Taig took her home.

"Thank you," Daphne said.

"Doesn't anyone bring you candy? Oh, these are pretty." Daisy admired a bowl of little daffodils.

"They're *Narcissus cyclamineus*," Daphne said, reading a card. "They're from the Taigs. Senior."

"They look like darling little clothespins! So why are you still lying down? Aren't you ready to get out of here?"

"If I stay here, I can see you every day."

"Can you go home?"

"Not yet."

Daisy took the Confucius out of her bag.

"What is that?" asked Daphne.

"This is what you bought me!"

"Do you like it?"

"I paid sixty dollars for it at the flea market!"

"I paid—" Daphne stopped herself. "A bit more."

"I've loved having it," Daisy said, "but you should take it back to James Rose. I hate to think what a 'bit more' would be. Why would you spend that on me?"

"Because you're Daisy. You're an integral part of our lives."

"Thanks," she said, smiling. "And you are of mine."

The Chantilly Box

1993

THURSDAY

Ew York streets are like discos. Catch the rhythm before stepping out on the dance floor.

West Forty-First Street was taking a break as Daisy Summerfield strolled east, eating a slice of pizza.

She arrived at the junk shop, wrapped what was left of the crust in a napkin, and went inside.

She saw a red-and-white patterned box that had four white spaces on the lid and four matching spaces on the bottom.

Ornamental fowl in blue, yellow, and pale turquoise were in the reserved spaces.

Holding it, she walked around the store, looking at everything.

The knob on the box was an ugly figure of Hotei covered with thick gold paint. A mark on the bottom of the box, a red hunting horn, was the famous mark of Chantilly.

Daisy could see and feel that the mark wasn't under the glaze. It was painted after the piece was fired.

She'd need to learn when Chantilly made a red mark over the glaze. It became common practice at some point in time for manufacturers to put their marks under the glaze as protection against people making imposters.

It was strange that no one had bought this box. The price sticker was old and dirty. If no one recognized the tiny painted mark, why was the box so expensive?

She took it to the counter.

"Hi," she said. "Does this have to be forty?"

"No." The woman put her greasy chicken back in its foil container. "I can make it thirty."

"Thanks!"

The bell above the door tinkled.

"Oh, so you came back?" the woman said. "Sorry, first come first served!"

To Daisy, the woman whispered, "He wanted that box but got very rude when I said we didn't take plastic."

"FIND SOMETHING you like?"

Daisy was fumbling with her money at the Murder Ink bookstore, too excited to make sense of the denominations.

"Calm down. Here, have a candy."

"I loved Mopsy," she said, choking on a butterscotch. "Sometimes she was a paper doll—"

Everyone was a detective these days, and Daisy was thrilled that one of her favorite comic-strip characters was appearing in her own new series. The first title was on the counter in front of her, *Mopsy: Trouble with Mr. Big.*

"Did you read the back cover?"

If you were one to agonize while cutting around the tiny wrists and tousled hair of Mopsy when she appeared as a paper doll in the Sunday comics, you'll be glad to know that she now works for you! Everyone's favorite cutie is now a

Private Investigator! The delicate windswept beauty attracts trouble like a magnet and repels it with a flick of a tiny red fingernail!

"I'm praying that it's good."
"When did it come out?"
"Last year. We're expecting the second one any day now."
"How did I miss it?"
"I don't know."

AS SHE washed the porcelain box, Daisy saw the Hotei had been re-stored. It was wet, so she broke off his head but didn't mind getting rid of old paste. She was going to spend the rest of the afternoon removing the restorer's paint.

WATER RAN noisily into her tub.

She stepped in and lay back with a sigh, admiring the raised red display type on the cover of her new paperback.

"Created by Gladys Parker."

How well she remembered the name!

With it came memories of Lake Minnetonka, the sound of wind in ancient trees, the glow of yellow light bulbs, card games, and the dream of creating her own comic.

Instead, she became a sculptor.

The shiny flexible paperback felt good in her stiff, work-thickened hands.

Mopsy, wearing a red suit with black lapels and cuffs, posed beside a desk.

A blurb praised the book's "warmth and humor."

Every day had been a red-letter day since Daisy stopped carving. Today she got this book and a box that might have been made by Chantilly. The factory opened in 1725 and closed in 1789 "due to the French Revolution."

Water covered most of her shapely, fifty-two-year-old body. She sat up, soaking her knees. She sank down, wetting her chin. Her faded blond hair floated in the water.

Putting her book and glasses on the sink, she shampooed and rinsed her hair. As she picked up her soap and washcloth, she thought she heard a noise.

"These old buildings make all kinds of noise," she thought. A familiar tapping started in the wall next to the toilet.

WRAPPED IN a towel and seated on the edge of the tub, she put on her glasses and picked up the book.

> "Whadda beeyutiful doll!"
>
> Dressed in the height of fashion, Mopsy sat unmoving in her desk chair.
>
> "Cripe," said the burglar, "it *is* a doll—one a them mannikins."
>
> He crept to the file cabinet, opened a drawer, and his big blunt fingers found the Weiss file.
>
> "Freeze." Mopsy pointed her tiny gun at him.
>
> "A talking doll!" he said.
>
> She pressed the button under her desk, and Lieutenant Ryan came in, smiling.
>
> Meanwhile, on the other side of town, a crook named Bug Eyes...

Holding the towel around her, Daisy stepped into her moccasins and went to look at her box. She looked on her desktop, window ledges, tool chest, and sculpture stands.

She thought she had left it on her steel bookcase but couldn't be sure. She went to her front door, turned the knob, and pulled the door open.

There was mail on the mat.

She picked it up.

Sometimes she didn't lock her door because she felt safe in her building.

But taking a bath with the door unlocked was unthinkable!

Where was the box?

"You look and look and try not to see it" was a saying of her grandmother. She thought losing things was exciting.

Daisy went back to the bathroom and shook her head. No, not in there.

Her phone rang.

She snatched it up. Taig had come, found the door unlocked, saw the box, and took it to teach her a lesson.

"Okay," she said, laughing.

"Daisy?"

"Daphne?"

"Who are you talking to?"

"No one."

"Should I call you back?"

"I lost something."

"What?"

"A box I bought at a junk shop."

"You'll find it."

She looked everywhere, eating the napkin-wrapped crust from her jacket pocket. The Hotei head was gone, too.

ACROSS TOWN, on Madison Avenue, two men were examining a Chantilly box.

"Where did you find this?" James Rose asked his finder—one of his sets of eyes in the City.

"Junk shop. Forty dollars."

"Looks very clean for a junk shop," Leon said.

The finder shrugged. "I gave you the short version. Do you want the long version?"

Leon and James looked at each other.

"No," James said, "that'll do."

He paid the finder for the box plus his fee.

DETECTIVE TAIG couldn't wait to see Daisy as he put his key in the lock.

She yanked open the door. "Did you take the little box I bought today?"

"No. What happened?"

"I went to a junk shop and found a little box and came home and washed it. Then I took a bath, and while I was in the bath, someone came in."

Fear gripped him.

"Are you hurt?"

"No."

"Did you see the person?"

"No."

"So you didn't come into physical contact with an intruder. Am I right?"

"Right."

High with relief, Taig picked up Daisy's copy of *Mopsy*.

"How can she read this crap?" he wondered.

"And I was having such a nice day," Daisy said sadly.

"Let's go and get some more books." Taig wanted her to be happy and liked to think he would do anything in his power to make her so. "Come on, I'll buy them for you."

The new *Mopsy* might have come in this afternoon. She would like to have it. This one was melting away like the butterscotch candy from Murder Ink.

FRIDAY

Daisy read mysteries in which female sleuths had police-officer boyfriends. Now she, too, had one, and he was as unhelpful as his fictional counterparts were to the women they loved.

She made magic for many people and longed for someone to make magic for her. Instead, she was on her own with a missing Chantilly box and Hotei head.

If a crazed collector stole it, the box was gone. She'd only had a glimpse of the man in the junk shop, but he seemed more like a shady business-type than a crazy Mr. Black. Who would someone, who was in it for the money, sell it to? There is a hierarchy. The dealer on the lowest rung sells to someone above him.

Daisy decided to start at the top and called James Rose. "I bought a Chantilly box yesterday."

"Do you want to sell it?"

"It was stolen from my apartment."

"I understand the feeling."

Daisy was hoping that wouldn't come up.

"Maybe you should move," James Rose added.

"I'll tell you what it looks like in case the thief tries to sell it."

"Fair enough. What was stolen?"

JAMES ROSE called the finder who brought him the Chantilly box.

"I think I need to hear the long version."

SATURDAY

A s Daisy walked up and down the aisles, she saw a flash of blue. "Those are bluebirds of happiness," Mr. Flea whistled through his stained gray beard.

The plastic birds were old and they wore little string harnesses someone had made for them. They looked like toys that had been in her crib, like birthday candle holders that she recalled from childhood.

They were the blaze of glory, the sunshine of the past, the crumby sweetness of the flea market.

Where were the psychologists, the sociologists, and the philosophers when such a rich subject was waiting every weekend on Twenty-Sixth Street?

Were the dealers hungrily seeking "the soul of things"?

Was she an empty vessel seeking other empty vessels? Or did she scent, with her long nose, something inside them?

"HE STOLE it from *Daisy Summerfield?*" Leon was aghast.

"He wants fifty dollars to put it back."

Was his father losing his mind?

"Fire him. Never deal with him again. I'll take care of the rest. This can't come back to us."

SUNDAY

For subway reading, Daisy picked Sheila Riddell's *Dated Chinese Antiquities 600–1650.*

It was one of Daisy's favorite books, particularly the section on zithers.

At the flea market entrance, she paid and had her hand stamped.

"Hello, Miss Summerfield," a dealer said, as she edged along his tables. She vaguely remembered him. "I'm sharing the booth today with a friend. He really wanted you to see something, but he just stepped away."

"Great, I'll stop back."

"We're building a house upstate!" He handed her a thick stack of photos.

She tried to turn several photos at a time, but he was looking over her shoulder at the many photos of a weed-filled lot.

He took them back and shuffled through them. "That lot right there is for sale. I can put you in touch with an agent."

"That's so nice of you!"

He loaded his van before dawn, drove for hours, and prevented people like Daisy from buying anything.

"I'll be back," she said, and escaped.

"WHERE HAVE you been? You just missed her!"

The dealer's friend, Tony, had gotten distracted by antique Amish wedding quilts at another booth.

Tony went to the pay phones, called Leon, and told him he'd try again next weekend.

THURSDAY

"What did you do today?" Taig asked.

"If you were Bug Eyes, you'd know."

"Who's Bug Eyes?"

"Mopsy's archenemy. His eyeballs are faceted, so he can see behind him."

"Okay."

"The second book finally arrived at Murder Ink. I said he was Mopsy's archenemy but he's really Chicago's—maybe the world's. The bad guys she catches are his agents."

"I had to go to the courthouse today," Taig said, yawning.

"Why?"

"I had to get permission to put a new sidewalk in front of my building."

Daisy had been to his place in Chelsea, and never guessed he owned the building.

"The other people are your tenants?"

"That's right."

She had rent stabilization. She paid a third of what a new tenant would pay, but her rent went up ten percent every two years, and she thought, "To live rent-free!"

FRIDAY

Daisy and Taig and Daphne and Alan met at the restaurant America on Eighteenth Street.

They were shown to a table.

A busboy put the bread basket near Daphne.

"What treasures have you found at the flea market recently?" Alan asked Daisy.

"When was Daphne going to pass the bread?" Daisy wondered, hungrily.

"May I have the bread?"

Daisy took a roll and handed the basket to Taig.

He handed it to Alan.

"May I have the butter?"

She broke her roll, buttered it, took a bite, and as she chewed her mood elevated.

There were vegetarian dishes on the menu. "I'll have pasta primavera."

They all chose pasta.

"So what about the flea market?" Alan asked Daisy.

"I was looking for something that was stolen from my apartment."

"It must be there," Daphne said.

"It's not."

"What are you reading?" Alan asked her.

She got the latest *Mopsy* from her jacket pocket, and showed it to him.

"Is it good?"

"It's great. I'm rereading it. As a kid, she made me dream of having a comic strip."

"What was your comic strip called?" Alan asked Daisy.

"You know."

"Tell me again."

"The Indelible Adventures of India Ink."

"What was its premise?" asked Taig.

"In her haste to push up the stopper and escape from the small black bottle, India Ink tipped it over. Now it has the power to blot her out forever!"

"Sounds psychedelic."

"She was always ahead of her time," Daphne said.

"Why didn't you send it to a syndicate?"

"I did. It was rejected. I was so desperate to leave home, I took the first thing I could find."

She and Daphne laughed.

"That's why we have midlife crises," said Daisy.

Daphne agreed with her. "That may be the reason for many failed marriages."

"You'd do anything!" Daisy cried. "Parents should be required to help their children go."

Taig was learning a lot.

SATURDAY

Daisy bought a porcelain scholar whose scroll had broken off, but his blue kimono and yellow gown showed the rainbow effects of age with no other damage.

Wearing a conical black hat, he was hurrying to show a friend a new poem.

"In your sleeves, more than ten new poems," wrote Po Chü-i.

The dealer wrapped him in newspaper and put him in a soiled plastic bag.

In the next aisle, she saw the home-builder and his friend.

He spotted her.

"Miss Summerfield!" Tony called, putting things out on the table.

She saw her box.

She picked it up. The Hotei head was inside.

"How did you get this?" she demanded, hoping he didn't have a gun.

"From another dealer," he said innocently. "Things go around, you know."

He looked nothing like the man at the junk shop who'd been rude because they didn't take plastic.

"This is incredible!" Daisy exclaimed. "How much is it? There's no tag."

"Twenty dollars and it's yours."

As Daisy bought the box for a second time, Tony suddenly found himself gazing at a goddess in four-inch heels held on by spaghetti straps.

"What did you get, my dear?" Lulu King asked.

She was so large and beautiful, Lulu attracted all eyes at the flea market. Her vintage eyeglass frames were copied by everyone since the spread on her in *Artgirl*.

"I just found a Chantilly box that was stolen from my apartment!"

Daisy read Swedenborg and believed the Universe was repaying the attention she gave it. But she also had paid for it twice.

"You have quite an eye for china, don't you?"

"No."

Lulu took her arm.

She and Daisy looked like soap opera stars.

Lulu held out her hand, fingers spread, displaying the costume diamond ring she just bought.

"That's great!" Daisy said.

"I saw you and the Kodalys and your sweetie at America. You were like a queen with her court."

"They treat me like a child."

"You are a child. I studied you at Pratt, and *I* feel protective of you. Do you like this?" She held up a velvet top from a table.

"It's synthetic."

"Do you always wear linen?"

"I love these shirts but they're expensive."

"May I?"

Daisy assented, and Lulu took the back of her collar and twisted it to read the label.

"Do you have time for lunch?" Lulu asked. "No, darling, not the coffee shop near your subway. You may not care about food, but I do."

Daisy examined the ring as they rode uptown in a cab.

"WELL?" SAID James Rose.

"It's done, and we are in the clear," Leon said, hanging up the phone.

THE RESTAURANT was nearly empty and they were immediately shown to a table.

Daisy was still overjoyed about finding her box.

"Isn't that all marvelous? Isn't the flea market wonderful? I told someone it was my art form."

"How often do you go?" Lulu asked.

"Every Saturday and Sunday."

Lulu studied the menu.

"When you say the Kodalys treat you like a child, do they say you should get back to work? Maybe they're right?"

Daisy trusted fellow artists. They had the mental toughness that got them where so many wished to be.

They didn't love art, they used it to explore ideas.

If they couldn't work big, they worked small.

If they lacked space, they did conceptual art.

"I've been showing since I was twenty," Daisy said.

"So what?"

"Art isn't art if you know how to do it. You agree, don't you?"

"Of course. But I think you take it too far."

"I got tired of seeing my name. It didn't feel like mine anymore."

"Marry Taig and take his name."

Daisy showed her the Chantilly box.

"Oh, it's fabulous!" Lulu exclaimed.

As Lulu went on about it, Daisy remembered the bluebirds she bought from Mr. Flea.

She imagined black or purplish stones set on white pedestals in the center of the Kodaly's smaller exhibition room, the dark broken by light around the bluebirds.

First she would carve the openings, then cut grooves, and fit Lucite sheets into the stone.

Lulu was still going on about each detail of the box but now it held little interest.

The Chantilly box was decorative, not fine art. Though it sat looking like a golden cake, it was manufactured and not the sum of an artist's breaths.

So, no, it wasn't fabulous.

Oh, the joy of working, the fun of saying, "I can't believe I'm doing this!"

The beginning: carefully removing chips to make the rough shape.

Maybe she could rent a studio if she worked large and got higher prices.

"And it's how old?"

"Could be early eighteenth century."

"Would you say that was a museum piece?" asked Lulu.

"I don't know. Maybe I'll take it to James Rose. Leave it on their doorstep, knock loudly, and run because I really don't care. You know Taig owns an apartment building in Chelsea."

Lulu pretended to faint.

"And you're, where? A place so small you have to sleep standing up?" Lulu asked. "If you don't marry him, I will, and I'll share the building with you after the divorce settlement."

"An artist needs security," Daisy thought.

How can she think what no one has thought, imagine what no one has seen, step out on the edge, without a safe place to return to?

Vincent van Gogh killed his brother with his constant demands for security. Jackson Pollock didn't make drip paintings until he was married to Lee Krasner.

"I don't know if I'd feel safe with security someone else gave me," Daisy said. "Taig asked about marriage and I said not before I'm sixty."

"Darling, you are the stern, older sister I always wanted," Lulu said. "How could you say that to him? He's a dreamboat! Apologize to him, get married, and start sculpting again."

They had finished lunch and were starting on their sundaes.

"But don't you think, when you look at a room full of art with your name on it, that it's all just nonsense?" Daisy asked.

"Daisy, darling," said Lulu, "we love the life!"

The Cute Bear

1994

SUNDAY

Antique china has value, but it isn't fine art. Like people, it is made of clay. Only art, architecture, literature, and music speak of the human aspiration to match the stars.

But still . . .

"We're here to learn how to choose," Daisy said to Daphne.

"I thought you were here to make sculpture."

"Maybe it's the same thing."

Standing before her open china cabinet, Daisy saw a world of objects that had something to say—a look, a style, a name, an address, a personality. She could banish one thing, bring forward another, put a third in the back row.

The old pieces she had found were gently scrubbed and rinsed by her.

The chips and cracks they had suffered were now part of their beauty after centuries of being knocked around.

Wouldn't it be great to be chosen by an artist like Daisy, and having been chosen, kept?

Wouldn't it be humiliating to be washed, dried, studied, and placed in a bag for the thrift shop, though others might see beauty where she didn't?

That is what happened to a former friend of Daisy's, a woman named Nancy Dick.

THERE WAS a miniatures booth at the flea market, Helen Smith's Small World.

Bent at the waist, her hands behind her back, Daisy studied the tiny worn furniture, dolls, and dishes.

She saw two women talking and called, "How much is the little green bowl?"

"I'll be with you in a minute," the older woman said.

Daisy paced beside the display.

"What did you want to see?" said Helen Smith. Daisy realized the other woman was probably her daughter. She looked like a forlorn mouse.

The dealer unlocked the case with a key, took out the bowl, and thought of a price.

"Fifty."

"No, thanks."

Daisy went on to the next booth, and examined the top half of a *papier-mâché* Easter egg.

"What are you doing here?" Nancy Dick asked Daisy.

"Flea-ing."

"Seriously. What are you looking for?"

Daisy hesitated.

If she were to say she collected china, Nancy would start collecting it, too.

Daisy said, "A rug, dishes."

Rug, she could see Nancy thinking. Dishes.

"Clothes."

It was spring, and both women wore nearly identical jeans and work boots they wore all year.

Blond, brown-eyed Daisy wore hers with a chambray shirt and a new denim jacket from SoHo. The pale blue flannel lining was printed with French comic-book characters.

Nancy wore a hooded olive-green sweatshirt. "Not a good color for you," thought Daisy.

"Maybe I should get a rug," Nancy said. "*Art View* might be coming to my studio."

Daisy was shocked but didn't show it. "What kind of work are you doing?"

"Geometric forms in stone and wood. They're abstract, but they represent events and people."

She was describing Daisy's art, but still Daisy gave Nancy good advice: "Just have white walls, clean floors, and your work."

"Really?"

"Yes."

Daisy squinted at an object.

Beside her, Nancy squinted, too.

"Are you getting that?"

"No."

Nancy took it to the dealer and paid.

"Want to get some coffee?" Nancy asked over her shoulder, but Daisy had already returned to the miniatures booth.

Helen Smith was berating the forlorn mouse again.

Daisy looked inside a case. A six-inch china-headed doll was lying on her back with a dagger in her chest.

Daisy angrily went to Helen, gestured at the case, and asked, "Why did you do that?"

"What?"

"I think it's sad. I bought a cup from a man who was stabbed here."

The dealer went to the case, fussily looked inside, seized Daisy's arm, and started screaming.

"WHAT HAVE YOU DONE?"

The market manager came running.

The dealer was keening.

"SHE DID IT!" cried the dealer.

A crowd gathered.

Daisy's eye was on the miniature dagger.

"What is that?"

Helen Smith calmed down and pulled out the dagger.

"It's jade," the dealer said.

Daisy was sure it was pale green plastic and had the words "Made in Hong Kong" impressed on it.

"I'm so glad I found it!" Helen said.

"I found it," Daisy said, hoping to get the green bowl at a discount.

The dealer was enthralled with her new toy, and the antique doll lay forgotten.

"Now, dear, did you come back to get the little bowl you liked so much?" Helen said to Daisy as if nothing had happened.

"What's the lowest price you can take for the dish?" Daisy asked the dealer.

Without even trying, Daisy had amassed a collection of miniature china. The lopsided cups, saucers, dishes, jugs, bowls, and teapots appealed to her.

She had seen iridescence on the green bowl, and thought it was the rainbow of age.

"I can't go lower than forty."

"Hi, Scottie," Nancy said to the forlorn mouse.

"We're working," Helen snapped. "That's my daughter, Scottie," Helen told Daisy.

Daisy thought, "She didn't look like a little black dog who could attack screaming like a Marine."

Daisy paid and dropped the bowl, now in a clear plastic envelope, into her pocket.

"Coffee? I'd really like to talk to you," Nancy told Daisy. "I miss hanging out with you."

"So do I!" It was Sam Wackhammer, a former police partner of Taig's. "Hi, Day."

Sam was with the manager, reacting to Helen's screams. "Everything okay here?"

"HOW ARE Darla and Carmel?" she asked Sam as they walked down to Twenty-Third Street, crossed Sixth Avenue, and continued west to the Fritzie Coffee Shop, a few doors before Seventh Avenue.

"Now, right there, that's a can of worms, Day," Sam said.

He was the only person who called her that.

"Why?" Daisy asked.

"What are you having?"

"Pie."

"I will, too."

"Maria wants Carmel to go to a private kindergarten. I say, then Darla should go to private school, too."

"Right!" said Daisy.

"Maria says Darla can get along anywhere."

"Why should she?"

"I can't afford two tuitions! Carmel needs special attention."

When Daisy met Sam's family, she was uncomfortable that Sam's wife so clearly favored their youngest.

"What kind of fruit pie do you have?" Sam asked the waiter.

"No fruit pie. We have apple, cherry, blueberry, and banana cream."

"I'll take apple."

"Two," said Daisy. "I got a book called *The Poetics of Murder.*"

"Poetry, eh?"

"They're essays. One says we read murders because *we've* been robbed and murdered."

"Uh-huh."

"That must be why so many women read and write them."

They needed more coffee.

"Waiter!"

"Though life's a mystery," Daisy said. "Did you ever consider being an artist? Sam Wackhammer is a great name for a sculptor."

Sam smiled and wiped the bottom of his freshly filled cup with his napkin, blotted up the coffee from his saucer, and set his clean cup in his clean saucer.

Daisy put her cup on her crumpled napkin and pushed the saucer away.

Sam said, "Maria wants Carmel to be like you."

Mothers often wanted their daughters to be like Daisy, and she always resented it.

"But probably better dressed."

THURSDAY

"How long have we been together?" Taig asked Daisy.
     "Two years."

"Do we have an anniversary?"

Her doorbell rang.

She went to answer it, saying, "Daphne was in a coma a year ago last spring, and it's spring again. So it's around now."

She looked through the peephole.

"Harrietta Taig," called a large woman on the other side.

"Mom, what are you doing here?" asked Taig.

"We stopped at Murray's."

Her short gray hair sprang from her head in a neat way and her hazel eyes were luminous. On the lapel of her tweed jacket was a silver brooch.

"Is that a Calder?" asked Daisy.

"I must have been inspired!" Harrietta unfastened it and handed it to her.

"Ma," Taig warned.

Daisy studied it and gave it back.

"No, keep it!"

"Where's Dad?"

"Finding a parking space."

"Come in," Daisy said, unselfconscious about meeting her boyfriend's mother. The Taigs were art collectors and had made hundreds of studio visits.

She held out the brooch and said, "Thank you for letting me see it."

"Let me pin it on you."

She attached it to Daisy's shirt. "Now you look perfect. Now *it* looks perfect."

Daisy's phone rang.

It was Taig's father asking them to come down.

Taig opened the door. "Sorry," he mouthed to Daisy.

"Let's go to the Pierre," Harrietta cried, as they approached the magnificent car.

Henry Sr., a head shorter than his wife and son, got out and embraced Daisy.

Then she and Taig were in the back seat, riding through Central Park.

"I don't have a jacket," Taig said, "and Daisy's wearing jeans."

Daisy wore jeans everywhere, but the large silver brooch made her feel like a sheriff.

"We'll get a suite and have room service," Harrietta called over the leather upholstery.

HENRY SR. put his napkin on the table and took Daisy's hand. "Who's your favorite artist?"

"Degas." She pictured the powdered and rouged face of a professional dancer waiting to go in front of the footlights.

"Really?"

"He's the most modern painter and the greatest sculptor. I like everything about him except—"

"Dreyfus."

"No, I feel sorry for him there. Degas was old and honorable. He wanted France to be right. I hate his sonnets and those letters about the white horse. I know who you like—Joe De Leo."

"Do you know him?"

"Very well."

"So how did you meet my son?" Harrietta asked.

"I love the flea market," Daisy began.

"So do I," cried Harrietta.

"And one day I bought a cup from a corpse."

"Fabulous."

"I asked if I could pay a dollar, and he nodded."

"That's great!"

"The next day I questioned her and knew I couldn't live without her," Taig said.

"I solved the crime!"

"What fun."

"It was a famous cup. Do you remember the cup that was stolen from James Rose Antique China?"

"Was that the cup?" asked Harrietta.

"Yes, and I accidentally knocked out the killer with one of my sculptures."

"That increases its value," Henry said. "Did you tell Alan Kodaly?"

"He would rather I were carving. I've solved five crimes, and the criminal—"

Harrietta asked, "How do you choose the criminal?"

"It's someone I dislike."

"Perfect."

"Is it true?" Henry asked. "Did you really solve five crimes?"

Taig moved his hand from side to side.

Daisy was outraged. "A Kodaly Gallery curator is writing about them!"

Taig shook his head.

This was intolerable. His parents liked and respected each other.

Henry put salt in the wound. "Do you know there's someone who copies your work?

"We saw it in a group show. What was the woman's name?" he asked Harrietta.

Daisy said, "Nancy Dick."

"You *know* her?"

"I taught her to carve."

"Pin a crime on her," cried Harrietta. "Put her behind bars!"

Daisy was falling in love with her boyfriend's mother.

DAISY HAD trouble unfastening the brooch and took out her books on Calder.

From the photos of his jewelry, she liked a rabbit's head formed by the initials MC. The fastening pin that was giving her trouble was piano wire, she read.

If she were an engineer she would make steel-ribbed collapsible fabric sculptures.

"You were really great with my parents," Taig said.

"Why wouldn't I be?"

"I can't always manage it."

"And yet," Daisy thought, "your mother is why you love me."

She and Taig washed up and got into bed.

She had thought it would be fun to have a romance with a detective before she knew about his background. She was an artist, her methods were undetectable. He didn't have a chance.

As she fell asleep, she imagined silk-and-taffeta sculptures supported by strips of bamboo.

FRIDAY

Daisy decided to call Alan and complain about Nancy Dick copying her work.

He said, "I think you should ignore it."

"I can't! She's the reason I stopped carving. Will you call her?"

"No."

"Calder said the artists who copied his work belittled it," Daisy said. "He tried to stop them."

"Daphne wants to talk to you."

"Why are you still carrying on about Nancy Dick?" Daphne asked.

"Art is hallowed ground! Rembrandt! Pollock! Filthy! Bloody! Fighting for their ideals!"

"You're her ideal."

"Art doesn't work that way! She'll be the death of us all!"

SUNDAY

Daisy saw a china fox terrier on a white oval base.

"That's eight," the dealer said.

"Where are you from?"

"New Orleans."

At a second booth, two frosted-glass dogs, a green pug, and a blue dachshund were six dollars each.

He gave her a price of eighteen dollars.

At a third, Daisy saw stained white miniature china in a cardboard box. She counted three plates, two saucers, a sugar bowl, a cup, a pitcher, a platter, and three lids.

The lids were as fluted and crusty as seashells.

"We dig that up," he said. "You wouldn't believe what people threw in their outdoor potties."

"How much for everything?" she asked.

HELEN SMITH was setting up her booth.

"You're Nancy's friend," Daisy said to Scottie.

"Careful with that box," Helen snapped at her daughter.

"I'm being careful, Mother."

Scottie set the box down and made another trip to the street.

"May I see the doll that was damaged?"

"Wait till I'm set up," Helen said as a woman in a brown coat approached her. "I'll give you a good price."

"DID YOU get the doll?"

"Yes."

At home that evening, Taig was being nice and showing an interest in her things.

"Is it here?"

She carefully took it from her china cabinet and showed it to him.

"So you bought this from Helen Smith."

"How do you know her name?" Daisy turned the key and reopened her cabinet to put the doll back.

"Helen died this afternoon. She was murdered."

Taig knew he should apologize for not backing her up at the Pierre, but he was giving Daisy something she'd like—a murder at the flea market.

MONDAY

Daisy took the doll from her cabinet, and a few grains of sawdust drifted to her oak parquet floor.

She decided to mend it. She had been given some tiny old needles by a young artist named Tamar Taylor.

The packet was one inch long, half an inch wide. She unfolded the black paper and selected a needle. At last she tugged it out.

"—and I can't believe what's happening—" said the voice in her ear.

Daisy was on the phone with Nancy Dick. She called to say she and Scottie were being questioned by the police.

"Which one of you two stabbed the doll? That was subtle symbolism," Daisy said. "I'm fixing the doll now, by the way."

Daisy had skeins of silk thread from a time when she wanted to do crewelwork. She took out the white and untwisted it.

Nancy was squawking on.

"I'm sorry to ask this, but I'm guessing Scottie was abused as a child? You know I think anyone who'd do that should be put to death," Daisy said.

Daisy selected a thread, cut it next to the knot, pulled it until she could feel the other knot, and snipped.

She put one end in her mouth, squeezed her lips together, and pulled it through.

She aimed it at the eye of the needle.

It touched the needle and bent.

"Why is she called Scottie?"

"It's her name. Everyone thinks it's short for something."

"Scottina?"

She wet the end, bit her lips together, pulled the thread through, and aimed it.

It approached the eye—and bent.

She wet the thread again, pressing it dry between her teeth, and set it down.

She had an old needle-threader.

Holding her cordless phone, she searched through her top desk drawer.

"Oh, wow," she said, as Nancy droned on.

She looked on all her bookshelves.

She found it in the wallpaper-covered cardboard chest next to her bed.

"Are you listening, Daisy?"

"Yes!"

She threaded the pointed wire loop and put the loop to the eye of the needle.

It was much too large.

She fell against the wall, defeated.

She cut the frayed end, and sucked on it, pulling it past her closed front teeth.

She put it to the eye of the needle, thought she saw it go through, and jerked her hand and swore.

"You know!" Nancy said. "They told her not to leave town!"

"Why?"

"They think she killed her mother!"

"Oh, right."

Daisy wet the thread again, aimed it at the eye of the needle, and brought it closer.

She saw a tiny fiber on the other side.

It was through. She pulled it farther. To be safe, she pulled it halfway.

"Tell me everything again," she said, and set down her needle and listened.

AT THE end of the day when the market was closing and dealers drove their vans into the lot, someone hijacked a van and mashed Helen Smith into the chain-link fence.

"Whose van was it?"

"Famous Attics."

While everyone screamed, the killer escaped through a hole in the fence.

No one knew if the killer was a man or a woman.

Nancy and Scottie were out on the street when it happened but no one saw them.

"At least Scottie didn't see her mother get killed," Daisy said. "Thank God for that."

She looked at the doll in her hands. Nancy, genius that she was, had symbolically accused Helen Smith of abuse and vandalized her property a week before she was murdered.

The edges of the hole made by the dagger were now neatly tucked in and Daisy was ready to start.

Starting with three tiny backstitches, Daisy sewed up the tear with a stitch called overcasting. She ended with three tiny backstitches and cut the thread.

Then she cut up a T-shirt, folded it, laid the doll on it, and traced a sleeveless dress. She cut out the two sides together, basted the seams, and tried it on her.

"Do you and Scottie have a lawyer?" Daisy asked.

"Everyone knows if the police question you, you need a lawyer. I only called you because your boyfriend's a detective."

"I've solved crimes."

"You're unbelievable! I don't believe you think you've solved crimes!"

TAIG CAME in while she was sewing.

Aware of the domestic picture she must make, she told him that Nancy Dick stabbed the doll.

"We need to tell Sam."

"Nancy is not a killer!"

After the way she and his parents talked about her, he thought that was strange.

"I'd have to kill someone first!"

TUESDAY

Daisy started searching for a *New Yorker* profile of Georgia O'Keeffe she knew she had kept.

It described the "uniforms" O'Keeffe designed for herself. They all had pockets.

Daisy had designed a series of clothes once herself and decided to sew them for the doll. All of Daisy's designs had pockets, too. It was more graceful than carrying a bag.

Calder had made jewelry for his sister's doll, and Daisy would make some for hers using the tiny glass beads and charms she collected.

She sorted through the charms:

- Mr. Peanut
- ice skates
- a baseball bat, glove, and ball
- a Chinese lantern
- a skull
- a primitive idol
- binoculars
- a spark plug
- a jackknife
- a boxing glove

- a white bulldog wearing a gold collar
- a white bulldog with no legs
- a skeleton missing one arm and one leg
- a compass
- a white glass mouse with minuscule bulging red eyes
- a photo of Gene Autry
- a photo of Roy Rogers and Dale Evans
- a *House & Garden* magazine cover that had a lakeside theme
- a harmonica
- an ocean liner
- a ring-toss game inside a plastic jug
- a megaphone
- a silver baby carriage containing a velvet blanket and quintuplets
- a 78 rpm Columbia record, "Your Heart's Turn to Break," Marty Robbins, flip side, "Out Behind the Barn," Jimmy Dickens
- a chartreuse hand dipping a chocolate-covered donut into a cup of coffee
- a souvenir book containing five photos of Llandudno
- four perfume bottles, two LILAC & two VIOLET
- a lobster
- a smiling green dog
- a roller skate

SUNDAY

Daisy was surprised to see the Helen Smith's Small World booth at the flea market.

An old woman with a brown wool coat was dithering with things on the table. Daisy remembered seeing her talk to Helen Smith.

"I have that little bookcase," she said, pointing. "I made books for mine and won first prize."

"I'm sorry about your mother," Daisy told Scottie.

"She loved Mrs. Tate's bear more than me," Scottie whispered, and tilted her head toward the woman in the brown coat. "She gave it toys and clothes, and had tea parties for it."

"Why did your mother have that woman's bear?" Daisy whispered, too.

The old woman might be the murderer!

Scottie checked to see that Mrs. Tate was far enough away.

Daisy could see why Nancy liked Scottie. She was a good whisperer. It drew the listener into an intimacy, but Scottie was just quiet.

"Mrs. Tate sold it to my mother a few years ago. Mrs. Tate was afraid when she died the bear wouldn't get a good home," Scottie whispered.

Scottie went to help a customer.

Daisy thought, "I have to see this bear."

If he was cute, she wanted him.

She could solve the case and ask for him as her fee.

"Do you know anyone who hated your mother?" she asked, after Scottie made the sale. Thinking of killers as infantile, Daisy said, "It must be someone who collects these things."

Mrs. Tate interrupted them.

"Your mother sold me a one-inch scale tea set for eighty-five dollars. One of the girls in my miniatures club showed me where 'Japan' was filed off. I was so embarrassed!"

"You can return it. Do you have it and the receipt?"

"No, dear. Everything is in Florida."

"If she lives in Florida, she must drive," thought Daisy.

"You can mail them to me," Scottie said.

"I'm not throwing money away on postage! I'll just take a few little things in exchange," Mrs. Tate said, filling a large shopping bag.

Daisy steered Scottie out of earshot.

"Where's the bear now?"

"Missing."

"And Mrs. Tate didn't ask about it?"

"No," Scottie whispered.

"You must be freezing!" Daisy said to Mrs. Tate. "I wish I lived in Florida and belonged to your miniatures club."

"You can't just *join* our club. We have to vote on your collection and miniature scenes."

Daisy was planning to make cardboard rooms and have her miniature china be the people. Partial sets would be families. Odd pieces would be visitors.

"How long are you staying in New York?" Daisy asked. "I know you were here last Sunday."

"I was not!" Mrs. Tate said too defensively.

Daisy excused herself and went through the exit to the pay phones, turning frequently to keep an eye on the woman.

She tried the precinct and asked for Sam. He wasn't available so she would take care of this herself. She replaced the receiver and stuck her finger in the change return.

The market manager stopped at a booth to collect their rent. Now he came up to Scottie.

"You want next Sunday?" he asked.

"Yes," Scottie said. "There's lots more to sell."

"There," said Mrs. Tate. The bag looked heavy. "Now just send this over to where I'm staying—and be very careful with it all."

DAISY ENTERED a red brick building in the East Thirties, walked through the sunken lobby to the elevator, and told the porter, "Nine, please."

He closed the gate.

Daisy had volunteered to deliver the bag to Mrs. Tate, and Scottie was happy to accept.

Daisy rang the apartment bell and heard footsteps. The outside hall smelled of something baking. Mrs. Tate opened the door.

"Special delivery!" Daisy said cheerily, holding up the bag.

She looked past a shocked Mrs. Tate and into the room. Daisy clapped her hands, and cried, "It's miniature!"

"Three-quarter scale. It's my friends' *pied-à-terre*. They use it when they come into the city. I just made some of my delicious orange muffins to leave for them. You can take off your coat and have some. I just need to add one more special ingredient, just for you."

Behind the sofa, a small table and two chairs had a view of East Thirty-Fourth Street.

On the table was a beautiful old Steiff bear, with a button in its ear. It wasn't what Daisy expected. It looked like a sad little girl. Daisy loved her.

"I'll just put on some water," Mrs. Tate said, going to the tiny galley kitchen.

"Didn't Helen Smith used to own that bear?" Daisy asked.

"Don't be an ass," Mrs. Tate said angrily.

"Is it for sale?"

"No!"

"I'm not leaving without her," Daisy said.

"I'm afraid you won't."

Daisy watched her open a cupboard.

She smelled chemicals.

The smell increased as Mrs. Tate brought a dish of muffins to the table.

"How did you make those in that tiny kitchen?"

"I can make my muffins anywhere, but I did have to use oven cleaner. I'm going to tell Elsie her cleaning person doesn't do a good job."

Daisy's eyes were tearing. She found a tissue in her pocket and blew her nose.

"I'm going to be hurt if you don't try some of my muffins."

Daisy took one, broke it.

"I want you to eat at least two."

"I'd love to take one with me."

She would take it to Sam and get it analyzed. Then he could come and arrest her.

"How did you know Helen Smith died? It's so sad," Daisy said. "I guess you changed your mind about the bear or she wouldn't give it back?"

"Have a muffin."

"I can't."

At first she thought Mrs. Tate was pointing at her with a silvery old finger.

"You have to eat two of these muffins and wait for the poison to take effect."

"You don't want to kill me here, there are too many police. Take me to Florida! I'll pay for it!"

Taig would see that her MasterCard had been used at Newark or LaGuardia.

"I insist you eat two of the muffins."

Daisy looked athletic, but she threw in a downward arc.

Taig said that the point of release was what mattered. Hold the ball lightly and let it release itself.

Daisy reached for a muffin, threw it, and hit Mrs. Tate on the arm.

She threw the next one too fast and missed.

She stood up and wildly threw the two halves.

She threw the last whole one, and heard something fall and smash.

Mrs. Tate turned to see the damage, and Daisy ran around the table and pulled her down and straddled her.

She wrested the gun out of her hand.

The grip felt warm and greasy when she put her finger in the loop.

"Get up and get in the bathroom," she said, kneeling on her back.

But she couldn't lock her in the bathroom. Bathrooms lock on the inside.

This was like carving. She couldn't make a mistake.

At this point in a sculpture, she would stagger to her bed for a nap.

She had to call the police.

Where was the phone?

Should she should run down nine flights and call 911 from the street?

Or should she go home and call Sam? He could arrest her in Florida.

The third choice was to do nothing, but she wanted the bear.

"Where's the phone?"

"I'm not telling you."

It was on the coffee table, in front of the sofa.

"Move back," Daisy said.

"No."

"I said, move back!"

Mrs. Tate stepped back.

"Keep going."

Mrs. Tate was near the door. She stealthily reached for the knob.

"Put your hands in front of you! Move to your left! Face the wall! Put your hands against the wall. If you move, I'll kill you!"

The coffee table was low, and she had to bend over to use the phone.

Daisy was very upset. She hated shouting.

She thought, "They have an apartment in the city, and this old push-button phone."

"FACE THE WALL!"

Daisy lifted the receiver with her left hand, put it to her ear, held it with her shoulder, and pressed 911.

"What is your emergency?"

"I'm holding a woman at gunpoint in apartment 9D," she said, giving the address.

"You're holding a woman at gunpoint?"

"Yes."

"We'll have a car there in five minutes."

"Thank you."

"OPEN UP!"

"I can't!"

Two officers broke down the door.

The one who took the gun touched her hand with cold damp fingers.

"He's nervous," she thought.

"The muffins are poisoned," she said. "May I give you my statement and go?"

"You're coming with us."

"There was a murder at the flea market on West Twenty-Sixth Street. Call Sam Wackhammer. Tell him you have Helen Smith's murderer."

"You can tell him."

DAISY GOT a cab down to Eighteenth Street, ran up the steps to America, and rushed to Daphne's table.

She took off her jacket, dunked her napkin in her water glass, and scrubbed her hands.

"What's wrong with you?"

Daisy took a trembling sip of Daphne's coffee. Using both hands, she set down the cup.

She hadn't been this tired since she had her first facial and didn't know how she would get home.

"I was late because I was fighting with a woman who had a gun—physically fighting with her. When I held the gun on her, the feeling was sexual. I had the power to blow her away. Now I know why sex and violence go together. People are disgusting."

She turned green.

"But art," Daphne said.

Daisy smiled at her.

She opened the shopping bag. "There's one good thing."

Daisy put the bear on the table. "I think I'll call her Charmie."

WEDNESDAY

There was a children's bookstore near the subway exit. A new book called *Paper Doll* was in the window.

"Let's go in and get books for Sam's daughters," Daisy told Taig. "Oh, I loved paper dolls!"

> Here is Edmonde.
> She has nothing to wear.
> Quick! a bathrobe,
> so she can at least sit around in it
> while we make her some clothes.

> She would rather wait in jeans
> and a T-shirt.
>
> We'll give her lots of T-shirts,
> some with a necklace.
> She has a pin she loves, too.
>
> She needs a suit to wear shopping.
> It looks fantastic with the T-shirts.
> Walk, walk, walk, walk.
> "How do you do, Edmonde?"
> "Hel-lo."

"That's for Darla," Daisy said, and opened the next book she found, *Sally the Teapot*.

> Sally the teapot was going out. "Which of my *chapeaux* should I wear?"
> She had a large collection of hats. Each one gave something new to her personality.
> Her spout was chipped and her original lid had been lost.
> She thought the chip was distinguished.
> "I'd rather be me," she cried inwardly, whenever she saw a perfect teapot with its matching lid.
> She kept her spout very clean, and was friends with a salt stick, a bread stick, and a dinner roll.
> The sticks shopped for baskets, and the dinner roll bought napkins to snuggle in.

Something smug about Sally made Daisy choose it for Carmel.

Daisy had thought of teapots as people, and so did this author-photographer.

And now, on colored pastel papers, came a group of *conté* crayons wearing berets in *Artists' Helpers Visit New York*.

"Get them all." Taig reached for his wallet. He didn't want to be late. But Daisy liked shopping.

THEY CLIMBED the steps to America, pulled open one of the large glass doors, and went in.

The last time they were there, Daisy discovered hush puppies with molasses. She couldn't wait to have it again with corn on the cob.

Maria and Sam's two little girls were up on the platform at the far end of the room.

"Darla is beautiful," Daisy told Maria. "Look at how graceful she is."

"Let me put a little blush and mascara on you," Maria begged Daisy.

Taig was filling in Sam about working for the DA's office.

"Sam says you solved another case," Maria said to Daisy. "You should have been a cop."

"I'm going back to sculpting. There's an old kind of theater the puppeteer wore over his head. I want to do that."

She remembered the Calder and peered into the V of her sweater vest. The pin was too valuable to leave in her apartment, too distinctive to wear on her sweater.

"What is that?" asked Maria.

Daisy stretched the V and showed it to her.

"That's nice."

Suddenly Darla was at her side.

"What's nice, Mommy?"

"Daisy's pin."

"Let me see!"

As Daisy was about to show Darla, fat little hands tore at Daisy's jeans, and a pudgy foot in a dirty shoe dug into her thigh.

Daisy showed it to Carmel.

Her little nose got red. Her mouth turned down. "Give it to me. Give—it—to—meeeeeeee."

"I can't." Clutching her, Daisy reached down for the bag.

"We brought you and your sister books. Look! It's a story about a teapot!"

Carmel slapped them out of her hand.

Holding on to Carmel, Daisy picked up the books and opened *Sally the Teapot*.

Carmel snatched at an illustrated page and tore it.

Calder would have made a toy for her, and another—a swan—for Darla.

"Darla," Daisy said, her face warm from leaning over, "we got you one about a paper doll."

"I don't really like books," Darla said.

"I've never seen you with kids." Myron Kantrowitz, a metal sculptor, stopped by their table and kissed Daisy.

"I waaant it," sobbed Carmel.

"She wants my brooch. Taig's mother gave it to me. It's a Calder."

"I want it, too!" Myron said.

"GIVE IT TO MEEEEEEEEEEEEEE," Carmel screamed.

Many people there had worse children and should have been inured to the sound, but some looked annoyed.

"Hey, kid. Take a look." Myron set the tines of two forks together and stood them up.

Carmel started to reach for them and Maria said, "I think she'll be a sculptor."

The Covered Jar

1995

TUESDAY

We arrived at Camp Ojiketa at 10:15.
I have a bunk under Miriam. everyone has gum and candey and we are all chewing. We had spagitti for Lunch, Stew for dinner. We talked till about 2 hours after taps.

We woke up today at 8:30 this morning and talked till nine. it rained so hard that we couldn't ride horseback. I started a coin purse at crafts today. For dinner we had cream salmon. We got to bed at 11:00.

D aylight was fading as Daisy sat in her Upper West Side studio reading her *Diary of a Camp Fire Girl.*

She didn't remember the red-and-blue book from her childhood. But she did have a dim memory of solemnly writing her Camp Fire name, "*Owa*, to paint, sketch," and making the symbol beside it (a hand and an eye) on the first page.

NATURE NOTES—
We went on a Hunt to find Mosquito's
Breeding place. We found it at the C.T.

We were all tired so we woke up real Late. We folked
danced in the Lodge and had Some Terrible tasting Orange
Punch or Something. We had Some Spagattie for dinner.

We got up at 7:30. I had 3 oranges for Breakfast.
We went to church at 10:00. The Biggest Island I ever
saw floated in. I went riding at 4-5:00. We had a
ambition party. We had Bloney for diner. Bed-11:00.

We got up at about 7:30 'cause I sneezed.
We had a hike. at night we had an auction. We
took Lodge duty. We had stew for dinner.

We got up at 7:45. After we cleaned
our cabin we went to handicraft.

NATURE NOTES—
We went on a Nature Hike and Saw a 15 min. old
Calf Learn to stand up. He did it in about half an hour.

She reached into the carton from her parents' basement and took out two binders, "Weeds" and "Leaves." The forty-five-year-old specimens still smelled good.

She opened a pink polka-dotted Storybook Doll box and found clumps of deckle-edged, black-and-white snapshots of her and her friends posing as glamour girls.

A key turned in her door. "What are you doing?" asked Detective Taig.

"Looking at things from Minnesota."

She put them back in the carton.

WALKING UP Broadway to the coffee shop, her jacket open in the mild air, she said, "At camp when I was eight, we had to take a salt pill before breakfast. We had to drink a cup of water with it. Here's what we sang when we drank it."

Drink your wa - ter with a will
Ho - dear - ie - dee
Ho dear - ie - a
Join us now and take your fill
Ho - dee - ree - dee - a - ho - dee - ah
Ho - dee - ree - dee - ah
ho - dee - ree - dee
ho dee - ree ah
ho dee ree dee ah ho dee ree dee ah ho dee ah.

"You seem to be enjoying your old things," he commented.

A FEW weeks earlier, Alan Kodaly had called.

"Are you working?" he asked.

Daisy pressed the phone closer to her ear.

He had good news, at least he hoped she would think so.

The Saint Paul Museum received a grant to commission a sculpture from her.

Daisy thought it was a horrible idea. Everyone would hate the sculpture because she was from there.

Alan didn't know his call upset her. She hadn't done a sculpture in the past ten years. He just thought this could get her started again.

Daisy pictured her old room at the front of her house. There was a white covered jar with a raised decoration on her bureau, a confirmation gift from Mrs. Price. Daisy had been thinking about it lately and wanted to have it.

Her parents would be in Florida, but she had a key.

It had been years since Daisy was in St. Paul. She thought it might be worth a trip to see how it felt after all this time. But really, she just wanted that jar.

WEDNESDAY

"You still haven't met our intern from Dewey. Her winter work term is almost over," Daphne said. "She's writing her senior thesis on your work. And she's the one who booked your flights."

"What year is she?" asked Daisy.

"Lara's a freshman."

"Where is she from?"

"California. She's staying with her grandmother on Park Avenue."

Daisy envied the privileged young girl.

"Lara can help you with your papers," Daphne said.

"They're private!"

"You still have to meet her."

"Maybe when I'm back from Saint Paul."

"You're going for a couple hours!"

Daisy's ambivalence about home was reflected in her travel plans. She was going and coming back on the same day.

"Hope it brings back strong memories," Daphne said. "Home will do that, in case you didn't know."

IN HER apartment, Daisy unpacked crayon and charcoal drawings she had made as a child.

Her parents had sent boxes years ago that Daisy never opened. Now she found diaries from her first two years of high school, beginning January 1, 1955.

Back to school tomorrow! After two terrific weeks of vacation, it seems pretty tough, but still, it'll be great to get back to Central

*High. I'm a Freshman there. I guess I'm still worn out from
New Years, 'cause I lost my temper about 3 times today. Once
mom slapped me for it. She's always wanted to, I guess, but this
was the 1st time she's ever gotten around to it! Oh-h was I ever
MAD! I talked on the 'phone all day today, besides drawing a
map for Civics. I didn't go down to the Bowling Alley, but the
kids said they saw Larry there!*

She read tensely, hoping to see that she had been intelligent.

*Well, it was great to get back to school, even though it wasn't
too great to start in with homework again! I have 10 algebra
problems and some Civics. I drive all my teachers crazy, 'cause I
talk so much, but they can't do too much about it, besides giving
me U's, and they don't!*

*You could never, in a million years, guess what happened to
me tonite! All of a sudden, while we were eating, I remembered
my map that I'm supposed to hand in to Mr. Gerspach tomorrow,
for Civics. I realized that I had left it at school. So-o, at 6:30
Daddy drove me down to Central. Only the basement door was
open, so daddy 'n I climbed 4 flights of stairs in the dark, found
my locker, and opened the combination by matchlite. It certainly
was an experience, especially when you realize that daddy
could've been arrested!*

*Well, I handed my map in to Mr. Gerspach this morning. I
sure hope I get an A for it, after all I went through last nite! Poor
Daddy... If I don't get a good mark, he'll probably shoot me! We
got out of school at 1:30 this afternoon, but most of the kids were
at the symphony, so I didn't do anything.*

DAPHNE HAD told Lara that she could work with Daisy, sorting old
papers. Now Daphne had to disappoint her.

"I don't want to go through her personal things," Lara said. "I just
like her sculpture."

She had brown eyes and curly blond hair. She looked like a young Daisy Summerfield.

> *Do you know what Larry did a few days ago?!! He got mad at me on the 'phone, 'cause I didn't understand a joke. So he said I should be playing marbles instead of talking to boys on the phone! I told him I'd be very happy to, but I didn't have any. The next day, he gave me 4 marbles. Now it's a fad! I think half the boys in Central have presented me with MARBLES! The recent count is—142!*
>
> *I'm reading a marvelous book now, called "Curtain Going Up." it's a really great book about Katharine Cornell—I've always wanted to be an actress! either that or an artiste! At any rate, I want to be <u>famous</u>!*

Daisy smiled.

> *We gave a skit about Egypt today in Mr. Gerspachs room. He really thought it was terrific! Oh well—there's no accounting for strange tastes! No kiddin', it was pretty good. It <u>had</u> to be! I wrote, directed, and acted in it.*
>
> *Bowled practically all day today. Everyone goes down to "Lucky Lanes" on Sundays! Everyone says I was just awful to, but I don't think I was! Sure, I was fooling around with all the boys, but I was with Gar just's much! I don't want to like only <u>one boy</u>! I like <u>everyone</u>! <u>I don't want'a hurt Gar's feelings, and I wouldn't for the world, but I don't want to GO with any one boy! I WON'T! I CAN'T!</u>*

How embarrassing. She was trying to sound like the teenagers in books she had read.

> *Just guess what happened at U High today! See—Gary took this picture of me from Mary's house. It's one of me acting silly,*

but anyway... they flashed it on the t-v system they have in the classrooms. It was on the screen for 'bout 5 min! Everyone's been calling me like mad! It is really pretty funny though, if you just think about it for a while—Just 'magine! It may be the start of my T-V career—hah!

We had conformation again after school. It's really very interesting. We discuss God and his existence, and learn to understand our Jewish prayers and customs! For next week, we have to write a theme on: "PROOF THAT I EXIST."

That reminded Daisy of the jar, the confirmation gift, she was traveling home to snatch up.

We had an awful test in BAND today, about scales, minor + major. I know I failed, so I'm not even thinking about it!

The PARTY was GREAT! I had the greatest time, ever! We Boped practically all nite, at least all the other kids did! After the first few dances, I gave up! Those kids sure can DANCE! 'Specially Merna and Connie! Gosh! I didn't know they were that good!

I'm just dead! (The day after the night before, you know). Mom wouldn't let me go Bowling today, because I talked back too much. Oh! She thinks I'm too tired too—(I am, but I'll be damed if I admit it!)

We had an assembly today, on SNO-DAY, which is tomorrow. We get to wear pants to school, and we get excused at 12:00 noon, to go out to Powder Horn park, for skiing, skating, etc.

Well... It was 19 below zero, so we decided not to go to SNO-DAY, but we got out of school early anyway. Oh well—If I'm expelled for skipping school, 800 others will be, too!

I got a darling pair of Kickerinos today! (real "HOODY") I got some ski sweaters, too, for the Sleigh Ride, but I'm going to return them...

I talked to Gary tonight for a while—he still has my mittens and angora hat from the sleigh ride! You see, I wore his jacket that night, and forgot to take that stuff out of the pockets.

I got a precious dress today. A Lanz! It's just adorable, for fla. I still haven't found a dress for The Sno-Ball. I talked to Gary for a while, tonite... Thrill-thrill-

I went downtown and had my hair cut in a "Sh-Boom." It's sort of motly! I had a marvelous time tonight. I didn't care for the movie too much, but...it was fun anyhow! (The movie was "Under Water" with Jane Russell) Afterwards, we went to Road Buddy's and had ribs—ugh!

I went downtown after school, and got a horsehair slip, a precious blouse, high heels, and pearl earrings. Mommy almost flipped, but she <u>did</u> let me keep everything.

THURSDAY

Daisy settled in her seat on the plane going from New York to St. Paul. While sipping tea from a plastic cup, Daisy read the second volume of her diaries.

I went to the dentists at 8:00 this morning. Susie was up there, too, and we went shopping after we had our work done. We went to absolutely <u>every</u> store in St. Paul, and all I got was a slip, sox, + a blouse! I lost Mum's cashmere sweater!! Wow!

I'm going out with Neil again Wednesday nite... We're going to see Blackboard Jungle. Um-m. Can't wait! (to see the movie that is)

Today was modeling—I take on Tues. and Thurs. at Comptons. We had an uneventful ride down on the bus (usually, it's hilarious) once this Bug flew on a lady—and—oh! Skip it! Anyway, today we had makeup first; that was really interesting...Well..not too, *but I had'a make it sound good. Then we had studio, and then wardrobe. Those wardrobe classes are nauseataing. All we do is take notes on how to wash bra's, how to fit girdles, etc. Ugh!*

I had such a swell time last nite. the movie was stupendous! Absolutely the mostest! I've never seen such a great movie. We went to a new drive-in, "Pearsons" - It'll take all the business away from "Flat top" and "Airloha." I sure could like Gary again - I used to have so much fun when I went with him. I went with Larry too - But now I hate 'em! Neil hasn't called...

I walked down to "Fines" (record store) and got "Story Untold" by the Crew-cuts! Wow! is that ever teriffic...

Oh- Last nite, when I talked to Neil I realized that I didn't like him anymore... I really don't think we should go together- we aren't right *for each other. We don't enjoy doing the same things, etc. At a party fr'instance: I can be having a smash-up time, But Neil'll be bored, and will mope around all eve. Oh- I don't really understand it, but tonite I made it quite clear to him. I hope he understands and his feelings aren't hurt. Also I hope that Gar still likes me, and that we start going together again. We sure go gr-reat together.*

I didn't do anything tonite, exept talk to Neil again, and try to make him understand...

A year or so later, Gary wrote from Wharton, "Physically, you're more beautiful than ever, and I seriously mean it. Mentally, you've matured."

The seat in front of her came back.

She said, "You're lying in my lap."

Went to Cooks, (I got a darling Italian "t" shirt) Murphys', Jacksons. As usual, we saw the whole crowd of freshman girls down there... those kids! They're all over! I bought three records at "Fines." 'Ain't that a Shame,' 'Close the Door,' and 'House of Blue Lights.' They're all real good.

Mummy + I argued for 45 minutes because she found some cigarettes I smoked, and she doesn't want me to smoke! I don't very often, but most of the other kids do, and I enjoy it! I smoke on the average of 1/4 cig. a day! Which isn't at all bad...

Daisy leaned back and gazed out the window at the quivering silver wing of the plane.

I walked down to the libe today, to take out some books. Gene Jones took me home... We talked for a while, and then he peeled away, in his little orange chariot.

Well- first of all, I've never had such a fun time as I did to-nite with Neil. the movie wasn't 'specially good ("The Man from Laramie") I really don't know what was so grand, but whatever it was... We went to the Flat top afterwards, of course, and had a long satisfying conversation about every little thing. I enjoy talking to him a lot. 'specially when he's in a bad mood- Then he isn't real scarcastic...

Sandy 'n I ate at the drugstore, and then went home... talked, read our new "True Confessions," etc.

This morning, I cleaned out my closet, bulletin board, and desk drawers. Whew! Then I cleaned my desk drawers for a second time (first was unsatisfactory according to Mom) Mary drove over. We went to the drugstore got some junk (Hot Coral Lipstick) and came home. Oh- We had a coke, too, of course... I talked to Neil tonite. I guess he's coming over tomorrow, but I won't be home... heh-heh

The woman on the aisle wanted to chat. Daisy said she was a scholar going to St. Paul to get a rare French jar.

"How did you ever get such a fascinating career?"

I went downtown today with Mums to get my little portable radio. it's 5" by 3", and so-o cute!! When I came home, I changed, grabbed my radio, and ran down to the libe. Oh- I'm reading "East of Eden" now, and it's just grand.

Oh! I got a just fabulous record . . . "Black Denim Trousers"!! I just love it.

It would be in her parents' basement, in a red leatherette carrying case of 45s she had indexed.

School started today! I got all crappy subjects, teachers, etc. You know how it goes...

A crappy day! I feel like I've been going to school for years already. it's just sickening routine. We have to collect 25 bugs, 25 leaves, 25 weeds for Biol. I have just tons of homework every nite. Lunch is my only bright spot, + I get indigestion from that!

Daisy rose and said to the man behind her, "Will you stop kicking my seat?"

She didn't see the man next to him. Would she have recognized her high school art teacher after thirty-eight years?

School was really bad- I got a real good study in Art, but I fluffed... it didn't turn out the way I'd planned...

Today was Sno Day- I get such a wierd feeling walking down the halls + seeing all the girls in downhills, bermudas, etc.

My! It's unbelievable, but school was worse than ever today... honestly! I just can not stand to take Art from Mr. French! he's an honest to goodness idiot!! besides looking like a gopher... ho hum... Well- I went to Ralph 'babe' after school and had my hair cut. What a relief! I looked like a zombie.

Got report cards en la escuela hoy, y ganno <u>All O's</u> in Wld. Hist.!! Muy Bueno?!! Si!! I also got a measly O in Art, and the rest were S's.

We had a bad assembly, no second period tho, so I didn't care. Mr. French looks more + more like a gopher every day. Gosh but I hate him! "Darlene can be very discourteous at times"... Duh-h-h.

I don't like Donny anymore. really! It's true... I really, really just think of him as a good friend, -n I want to date him some more, but this is the end of the "Darlene loves Donny" saga. I'm going out with Gar tomorrow.

We had a real fun time tonite. went to see 'I hear America Singing' at Central. It was extra fabulous!! After, we went to <u>White Castle</u> + it was just a panic, + Oh! We went to the High. theater for the last 15 minutes of the show... Gar said: "Let's walk in backwards and they'll think we're leaving." hm-m..

She remembered Gary and that moment but very little else. She always thought her life was a book she would read one day.

Then we drove all over town + Gar let me steer. I ran up on a curb...

Inability to control a vehicle was a female trait in the fifties, but Daisy was a good driver.

Tonite was grand! Sandy + I went to the mixer. We saw Donny there, he kept fooling around with me, Sandy hates me, etc. Donny took Suzy, Sandy and I home, but he took me last, and we talked in the car for at least 1 hour. I told him about everything that'd been going on tonite, and he told me just how he felt about everything, and why he didn't like sandy, why he liked me, etc. he asked me to the Pow wow... hurray!!

She did remember thinking that dating was her job.

"I always take things seriously," she thought, "including being a teenager."

Sandy came over. She feels awful about Donny, but geeze! What can ya do about it? The whole town's talking about how I got Donny, etc. All he did was ask me out. I don't go with him...

Went to the Central-Wilson game tonite. We won 27-0! It was a swell game- Larry played 1st string! I was so proud of him.

O happy day! Donny asked me out for tomorrow nite. We had a test in Biology too, + I think I passed, because Dave really studied hard.

We had the most wonderful sub. in Biol. today! he was about 21, dark curly hair, glasses, buck teeth, etc. I'm in love-e!!!

We had more tests in Wld. Hist. today, and Mr. French wrecked one of my best watercolors. My, but I hate him!!

They came out of the clouds, and she alone applauded the tree-outlined fields and brown river before they landed with a bump.

She was out of her seat, exposed to the two men she had humiliated.

"Good luck with the jar," said the woman from her row, now standing behind her.

"Thanks." Daisy quickly looked away.

She had seen her high school art teacher, Eustace French.

The new airport was constantly growing, and she had to follow signs to a cab stand.

Her parents always picked her up.

She opened the door of a cab. It was filthy. Could she refuse to take it? The Midwest was supposed to be clean! She got in, put her backpack in her lap, and gave the driver the address.

She left the window down a crack, loving the freezing air. It was so nostalgic. She wished she had more time.

She could have pizza at Carboni's, and the Barnes & Noble carried books of local interest.

It was a short ride.

"I'll tell you where to stop," she said. "Right . . . here. It's this house on the right."

DAISY OPENED the back door and stood facing the basement stairs.

It felt strange being alone in this house. She was used to people above, below, across from, and beside her, irritating though they might be.

She went through the kitchen and over the landing to the living room.

In the front door, she pulled on a little wooden door and put her hand in the freezing metal chute.

Her college acceptance came through that door and led her to a wider world.

DAISY OPENED the kitchen door, found a can of mixed nuts, and went upstairs chewing.

The covered jar wasn't in her bedroom, so she went down to the basement.

As she went upstairs again the phone rang and she hurried to her parents' bedroom and picked it up.

"Who is this?" a familiar voice asked hesitantly.

"Dad?"

"Wait, did I call New York?"

Standing in her parents' bedroom, looking down at the street, she saw an old blue car.

She said, "I'm in Saint Paul."

"Gosh, I thought I was losing my mind! What are you doing there?"

"The Saint Paul Museum wants to commission a sculpture."

"That's terrific!"

There was only one phone in their motel room. Daisy waited while he told her mother.

"I don't know if I'll do it," she said to him.

"When did you get in?" he asked.

"A few minutes ago."

"How long are you staying?"

"An hour. I wanted to make it quick."

"Make sure you lock the door," her father said.

"I will."

"Is everything okay there?"

"Yep."

"How's the weather?"

"Freezing."

"What's the temperature?"

"Why did you call here, Dad?"

"Just checking!"

He gave her mother the phone.

"Mom, may I have two of your old towels?"

"I'll send them to you when we get home."

"Do you remember a white covered jar Mrs. Price gave me that was on my bureau?"

"It was a pewter box."

Daisy went to the bureau and there it was. Pewter. She had no memory of it and it meant nothing to her.

Daisy chose two towels and went downstairs.

The enormous green furnace was gone! She found another carton of her things.

The candy box that contained the teenage paper doll she had made wasn't in there.

Upstairs she saw by the kitchen clock that her time was running out.

She looked around the house, trying to feel some emotion, but she hadn't lived here long as a child. The old house in Mound, thirty miles to the west, buried in lilacs on Lake Minnetonka, was another story.

Blanche Nichols Wilson wrote in *Minnetonka Story*:

> How often I heard "By the Waters of Minnetonka" pouring from bus station and airport juke boxes during my visits in the South, I cannot say. Almost always the majority of the travelers who had given little heed to previous records, be-gan to listen to the rippling of the waves and the longings of the human heart expressed in that pensive melody. One time a pretty WAC near me gave such a tremulous sigh that I asked by way of sympathy, "Where is Minnetonka?"
>
> She gave me a sad look, grieved at my ignorance. "Oh, it isn't anywhere. It's just an imaginary place, sort of a Shan-gri-La, you know."

Daisy had made and colored the teenage paper doll and her large wardrobe at the dining table on the porch.[1]

The old lake house was no longer there. The lakeshore was now filled with ugly, lavish houses of the wealthy, all pressed together.

---

1 In 2005, Daisy was inspired by playing Solitaire on her cell phone.

The moment took her back to the porch at the lake, and she invented a game with four rectangular dolls.

Their clothes were dealt three at a time. The object was to outfit all four dolls.

Daisy had gone there years ago and she couldn't even find a way to walk by the water. It had broken her heart.

DAISY GRABBED her old slam books and a little blue flight bag for the two towels.

Her cab drove up.

The back door of the house was locked. She locked the front door, tested it, and went down the icy walk.

She thought she saw an old blue car through the rear window when she turned for a last look at the house.

THERE WAS a woman in the middle of her row. She had a bandaged foot and a cane.

Daisy opened a bin and put in the flight bag and her jacket.

"Aren't you Darlene Summerfield?"

"Yes!"

The woman looked familiar.

"I don't know if you remember me from Central High. I'm Carol Hanson."

The former Sno Queen was the same as when she said hi to everyone in the halls of Central.

"Welcome aboard your Northwest flight to LaGuardia," said the pilot. "Our flying time today will be two hours and thirty-five minutes."

"How did you hurt your foot?" Daisy asked. "Is it an old cheerleading injury?"

"No." Carol dimpled. "I had surgery. Our daughter, Melissa, is a dancer with the New York City Ballet."

"Neat!" Daisy said. "Who did she study with at home?"

"Katy Parker."

"I took ballet from her!"

"They said they couldn't teach her after she turned twelve."

"What did you do?"

"Melissa and I moved to Chicago, and my husband and son stayed here."

They were flying above the clouds. By "here," Carol meant St. Paul.

"When she was fifteen, we let her go to the School of American Ballet. I've been going on and on, and you haven't told me about yourself," Carol said.

"There's nothing to tell."

The short man in the row ahead disagreed.

"Are you married?"

"No."

If Daisy had talked about Taig, things might have been different. Carol asked for a pillow, and Daisy opened her diary.

> *I went downtown today, to see the "Benny Goodman" story. It was fabulous! The music was... the plot wasn't so hot (hah-hah) that rymed!! I'm so origional tonite.*
>
> *School's getting just ridiculous!! I have to stay after school for Mr. French tomorrow, and I think I'll tell him exactly what I think of him... My name'll be on the Suspension list Friday, probably... I <u>hate</u> that man (not man, mouse or rat is more like it)*
>
> *I had to stay after for Mr. French today. he gave me a big lecture about how I'm wasting my glor-rious talent in art, and how much better I'd be if I <u>worked</u> instead of fooling around with Bill and Tom. Phooey!*
>
> *Gosh but I hate school! Only 103 days left, counting weekends. I'll live. Stan + I counted the days in Biol today, 'cause we had nothing better to do.*
>
> *I had another whopperoo of a fight with Mr. French 'babe,' + did a <u>really</u> good portrait of Margie in art today. no matter <u>how</u> Mr. French hates me, he has to give me a 4+ on it!! he just has to...*

"WELL, IT was real nice seeing you. I meant to ask, what were you doing in Saint Paul?" Carol asked. "Do your folks still live there?"

"Yes," Daisy said, as the plane landed.

She closed the lock on the white leatherette diary and put it in her backpack.

The plane came to a stop.

"Thank you for choosing Northwest."

"As if we have a choice," she always thought.

She saw Eustace French open a bin and take her flight bag.

Trapped because of Carol, she could only shout, "Hey!"

"Excuse me," she called to the young man sitting next to Carol. "Someone took my bag!"

"Will you let me out? It was nice seeing you," she said to Carol, getting her jacket.

Her high school art teacher had stolen her towels!

Daisy raced into the terminal.

She went left and then turned back and went right. A crowd was forming. Her first thought was something she read in *People* magazine. An article said Dolly Parton was always in airports and was very short and friendly.

Daisy tried to see her.

Instead she saw a pathetic blond woman, wearing the same color coat as Daisy, lying on the industrial carpet. Two police officers were nearby.

The police helped the woman to her feet. There was blood on the back of her head where she'd been hit.

Daisy accosted a police officer.

"What's the problem?" he asked.

"I think I know who did it."

He said, "This is drug-related."

TAIG THOUGHT it was drug-related.

"Why can't you believe my high school art teacher attacked and maybe tried to kill a woman he thought was me!"

He stared, trying to figure her out.

FRIDAY

B uy and donate. Buy and donate. Paula Conrad cut a swath through the material world.

In every corner of the city where she taught reading, she went into a store and bought something.

"How's your work?" she asked Lara, as they sat down at the dinner table.

"Fine, Grandma."

"Sweetheart, could you call me Paula? I don't like a generic name at my age. Are they still giving you good things to do?"

She helped herself to Mushroom Stroganoff and passed it to Lara.

"I'm still cleaning out old files. They let me keep a lot of cool stuff. What was Philip Kodaly like?"

"Very stern like Mondrian. Did you know Philip Kodaly was there when Summerfield had her first show?"

"Yes. I wish I'd never mentioned her, though. Daphne keeps bugging her about me."

"Sweetheart, I don't know Daphne, but she does what she wants to do. And Summerfield will do what she wants to do. I could invite her here."

Paula hadn't spoken to Daisy since their first semester as freshmen roommates in 1958. It was a lifetime ago, and Paula was secretly afraid Daisy would have forgotten her.

"You said you really didn't know her at Dewey," Lara said.

"She can still come and eat potato latkes and see her *Gettysburg Witness*."

"Does she know you have it?"

Paula had excused herself from the table and was searching her bookshelves.

"I would doubt it. Back then we used an agent. Here. Wipe your hands. This is the catalog for the first show of Witnesses."

Lara took the gray paper-covered booklet and opened it.

Daisy Summerfield, born in Mound, Minnesota, on Dec. 21, 1940, attended Dewey College in Vermont before coming to New York.

There was a photo of her in a striped Mexican-style blouse and dangly silver earrings.

Paula had stepped into a life she couldn't have imagined if she hadn't gone to Dewey. She wondered if Daisy felt the same.

"Did you know she solves crimes? The Kodalys hate it, because the criminals are curators or dealers."

Paula laughed. "No, I didn't know. But if I were still painting, I'd have it in for them, too."

"I think she has a really deep reason for doing it."

"Laraleh—"

"What did you call me?"

"That's a love name. I hope you write down the things you say. They're good insights for your paper."

"I think it's interesting that Daisy's never been married or had children."

"If your mother didn't have you, I don't know what I'd do. You're a better miracle than any artwork."

Paula considered the limestone *Gettysburg Witness*. The stone was very delicate.

"We were lucky to get this," she said. "Our first two choices were sold. *Spottiswood* had two peaks and was spotted with black paint. The other was a marble column with a pointed roof, and on the roof it said 'Grant.'"

"Why did you stop painting?" asked Lara.

"I was too happy!"

Lara went to her room to get ready to go out with friends.

The Yiddish diminutive, Laraleh, had slipped out. It brought her grandparents so vividly to mind.

They had sold their house at Minnetonka before moving to California in the early 1950s. What she wouldn't give to see them again!

SATURDAY

On one of the tables in a large booth at the center of the antiques lot, Daisy stopped to look at a porcelain rooster. Then next to it she saw the jar she had gone to St. Paul to find.

According to her mom, Mrs. Price had given Daisy a pewter box. This jar, though, was what she remembered: white and lidded, decorated with a raised design of prunus blossom.

There were bronze rims around the bottom of the lid and the mouth. "Added," she thought.

Holding the tiny knob, she removed the lid and put it back. It fit precisely.

Large initials, "DV," were incised on the bottom.

She bought it for fifteen dollars.

DAISY FOUND the initials in W. B. Honey's *French Porcelain*:

> The mark 'D V' (for 'de Villeroy') was used from the beginning on Villeroy porcelain. It was at first, apparently for a short time, painted, sometimes in blue (like Saint Cloud), more often in red (like Chantilly). For the most part, however, it was incised in the paste, sometimes accompanied by the initials of throwers or 'repairers.'

She examined hers, and saw two curved *C*s back to back.

She checked *Pottery and Porcelain* by Warren E. Cox, which showed a covered jar like hers.

There was much further talk of places, pastes, and glazes and then this paragraph she loved:

> Here we see that even in the early days of the eighteenth-century creative spirit had become so atrophied that factory copied factory and there was no slightest respect for the rights of personal design or desire to cultivate it. One small bright idea was dragged from place to place until it was worn to pieces.

SUNDAY

Taig paid their admission, and Daisy went to find the rooster.

It had stayed on Daisy's mind and she was convinced she'd lost it to someone else, but there it was. His tail was broken, his comb was chipped, and someone had painted pearlized nail polish on it.

She looked up and froze.

"That's him!" she hissed to Taig.

"Good."

"My high school art teacher! The man who stole my bag and hit that woman!" She punched Taig's arm.

"JESUS!"

A crazed Mr. French hit Daisy on the head with her flight bag. Fortunately, nothing heavier was handy.

"What are you doing?" Daisy screamed.

"Police," she heard Taig shout.

"I can't go through this," Daisy thought, and fainted.

SHE AWOKE on the floor of the parking attendant's hut, next to the entrance to the flea market.

As an admirer of Chinese and Japanese poets, who all loved huts, she looked around with interest.

If she took away the desk, there would be room for a bed, a stove, and a lamp. She could hang a shelf for books.

"Is the rabbit in my bag?" she asked Taig.

"Rabbit?"

"The white porcelain rabbit would be her sole ornament," she thought, sitting up.

Like Ryokan with his vase, she would keep it dust free.

WHEN AN officer had dropped her off, she unwrapped her package and was surprised to find a rooster.

"Why did I think it was a Japanese rabbit?" she wondered.

DEE, DEE, *dee, dee, dee, dee, dee,* went the lighted pads on her new cordless phone.

"Hi," Daisy said.

Daphne was happy to hear from her. She said, "Lara's grandmother owns your *Gettysburg Witness*! I just found out. She was in your class at Dewey, and she's from Minnesota! Her name is Paula Conrad but it was Nathanson."

"Are you sure? That doesn't sound right. I want to read to you from my high school diary . . ."

> *I went to modeling today at 1:30. My first professional class...*
> *fun! By the end of summer I'll be a full fledged professional*
> *model! The girls in my class are nice.*

> *I went to modeling today & guess what? I got a job!!*
> *Modeling at Donaldson's for the Aquatennial! $1.50 an hour, &*
> *Mom bought me a beautiful models hat box at Daytons...*

> *I went down town with Carole today. I got Harry Belafonte's*
> *new record "Calypso." It's really good...*

*I went to the doctor's for my second polio shot + on the way
to the Hairdressers I got off at the wrong place so I walked about
5 miles + then I saw Gene Jones in front of his house so he took
me the rest of the way... Jimmy called a few times while I was
out having my little adventure -*

*Nancy + I took the "Special" bus home from school today,
changed + then Nan picked me up + we went horse back riding...
fun! We rode at Ding's ranch + the horses are really great! Oh-
h, it was just heaven!!! We're going every Monday from now on.*

*Nan + I took the "Special" home from school again today.
Then we changed + went horseback riding out at Ding's again.
I improved a whole lot + I just had a grand time! I learned
to slide off the back of the horse + how to saddle + unsaddle
Buckskin Lady etc. Fun!! We rode real hard + I don't think I'll
be stiff tomorrow...*

"I didn't know you rode a horse," Daphne said.
"Isn't Buckskin Lady a great name?"

*I hate my parents - I never want to see them again - I'll run
away - (I wrote that this morning. I still hate them but I think
I'll stay home + make them miserable instead.) I hate my
mother because - well - Daddy takes my delinquent neighbor to
school every day. I won't be seen with him so I just thought I'd
take the bus. Dad and Mom got mad etc., I talked back to them
+ now I'm not allowed to go anywhere.*

*I was going to eat at Bill's house tonite + Mrs. Peterson was
expecting me + everything... but... MOM!!! Mom wouldn't let
me go...*

*I took my Spanish I + Wld. hist. finals today + then Meta got
the car + we all went to the Beach. I just had a ball with Bill +*

*Dean. Bill + Harley were out there too, but I guess Bill + I aren't
on good terms or something... I went out with <u>Jimmy</u> tonite. We
saw "Carousel" at the Highland. Mom, Dad, Vic, Tari, Susie,
Jane were all there too... then we went to Flat Top + came home!*

*Tonite we really had fun. Nan + Tari went driving with
Susie + me... We ate at Flat Top + then we drove all around
singing in harmony.*

"What do you think?" Daisy asked.
"Are you sure you didn't buy it at the flea market?" Daphne said.

MONDAY

Throughout this week, our story's characters were like Su
Tung-P'o's "little stars busy as boiling water."

Taig questioned Daisy's old art teacher and let him return to St.
Paul; Daphne wrote her report: "It was a joy to have Lara Cooper at
the gallery. In cleaning out old files, she demonstrated a real understanding of the relationship between art, academics, and trade"; and
Lara called her friend Stephanie to arrange her ride to school.

FRIDAY

Daphne pressed Play on her answering machine.
Daisy's woody voice said, "Daphne?"

If I were a bunny
with a tail of fluff
I'd hop up on your dresser
and be your powder puff.

Daphne rewound the tape and called Alan. "Listen," she said.

"What is that?" he asked.

"Daisy! She's still going through her old papers. Sounds like something from an old autograph book. Isn't that a sweet message?"

She hoped he wasn't jealous.

"She couldn't say she wanted to be *your* powder puff," Daphne. "You can ask her about it tonight. Remember we're seeing her with Lara."

"Who?"

"The intern! It's her last day."

DAISY WAS making a slam book.

She turned over the first page of an unused sketchbook and wrote at the top of the second page, FAVORITE SCULPTURE, & SKETCH IT IF YOU CAN.

The heading for the next page was, FAVORITE PAINTING, & SKETCH IT IF YOU CAN.

> Favorite song
> Best kind of music
> What kind of soap do you use?
> Brand of toothpaste?

"Tom's," she wrote.

> Your favorite shampoo + your hair type
> Have you ever had a great haircut? Where and when?
> Are you doing what you set out to do?

"No," she wrote. "I was going to be an actor!"

> What are your favorite clothes?
> Who are your favorite artists? Reasons?
> Favorite photographer

Lee Friedlander. See "Wade Ward's Granddaughters."

If you could choose your talent, what would it be?

Do you have a cat? What's his or her name?

Do you have a dog? Name, please.

Would you rather make money or inherit money? Please
be thoughtful & give reasons.

Forget sanitary conditions, penicillin, etc., and say when
you would have liked to live, & why.

Do you wear glasses? Draw the frame & note color(s).

Favorite fashion accessory.

Favorite jewelry. Do you ever take it off? Why? Why not?

Do you reinvent yourself? Does it last?

Do you ever completely change the contents of your
apartment?

Where do you live? Describe.

If you could move, where in NYC would you like to live?

Are you a native New Yorker? If not, where are you from?

Do you still have an accent?

Daisy answered, "When I'm lonely."

What does it sound like? Choose a word or phrase and
spell it out.

"Theynk yaw," she wrote.

Do you remember yourself as a child? An adolescent?
A teenager? A young adult?

Do you wish your young self could see you now?

"Yes."

Favorite movie

"The Umbrellas of Cherbourg."

There was no room for favorite author, favorite book.

"Artists don't read," she thought recklessly.

She turned back to the first page, headed, NAMES, PLEASE, to start numbering down.

In the old days, you would take a number and write anywhere on a page. She thought of an improvement, and went back and drew triangles around her answers.

"DID YOU know Daisy was a Commercial Girl in high school?" Daphne asked Alan on their way to the restaurant.

"What's that?"

"It was a line of pretty girls wearing dresses with crinolines chanting commercials at assemblies.

"I told Lara we'd pick her up, but she said she'd meet us there.

"There she is! Hi, Lara!" Daphne cried, getting out of the cab in front of America.

Alan gave his name to the receptionist, and they were seated at the far end of the hangar-like space at a table under the skylight.

"WRITE IN my slam book," said Daisy.

"What's a slam book?" asked Lulu King. She was in the restaurant with Rudy Shayne.

"Just follow instructions," she said pertly, as Taig pressured her shoulder.

From their table, Daphne, Alan, and a young blond were watching their progress.

"Daisy and Taig," Daphne said, "this is Lara."

"Hi," said Daisy. She picked up her menu and said, "Lulu King and Rudy Shayne are writing in my slam book. Instead of taking a number, you choose a shape and draw it around your answers. I have to see if they're doing it right," she said, and got up and left.

Taig tried to excuse her.

Daisy went table hopping, telling everyone she knew that she had made a slam book and asking them to write in it and how to do it.

Alan was furious.

Taig said, "She's just letting off some steam. Her high school art teacher assaulted her with a flight bag at the flea market."

Daisy sat down.

"Are you mad at me?" she asked Alan.

"Yes. You're being rude."

"This is how I was in high school."

"No wonder your teacher wanted to kill you."

She looked down at her menu. The more she willed herself not to cry in front of the young intern, the more painfully her eyes smarted.

Lara wanted to disappear.

Daphne thought, "It's true. He's in love with Daisy." She wanted to get up and run out of the restaurant.

"What's going on?" Taig wondered.

Alan said, "I apologize. What do you think about the offer from Saint Paul? Did going there help you think about it?"

RUDY HAD drawn phalluses around his answers. He couldn't draw, but the shape was unmistakable.

Lulu tried to counteract him by outlining a Christmas angel.

Under "Best Haircut" she wrote inside her angel, "On the beach at Nice, winter of '75, 5 fr."

Rudy's best haircut, inside the phallus, was "When I was on *Guiding Light* in the '60s."

Daisy's triangle contained "Jon-Allen, Bendel, Dec. 1975, when Jean Louis David was giving free haircuts."

Daisy wished Jack Katz was there to sign it. She'd get it to him. And Myron Kantrowitz, Joe De Leo, Linda Leone, and Mr. Flea.

"What shape will you use?" she asked Taig.

He took out his pen, turned back to the first page, drew an outline of a police badge, and printed "Henry Taig Jr."

So far, Daisy was the only one who had used a geometric shape.

"Hepworth's sculptures still look good," Daisy told Daphne and Alan, handing Alan the book.

"Where's that coming from?" asked Alan.

"I mean, they aren't dated. I was subtly suggesting using shapes like hers."

Alan drew an uneven circle.

"Wow," she said. "Are you sure you can repeat it?"

It was the sun, signifying his continued interest in the Impressionists.

Daphne didn't know what shape to choose.

Daisy asked Lara to write in it, but Lara refused.

"I could draw a cloud," Daphne said. "No, I'll draw a cat."

They ordered coffee and dessert and passed the slam book.

UNDER FAVORITE Saying, Daisy wrote, "Music of the spheres."

Rudy wrote, "Dumb as dogshit."

Alan wrote, "I have a Monet Haystack I want to sell."

Daphne wrote inside her cat shape, "NO MORE DETECTIVE WORK."

"That's not a saying." Daisy ran around the table, reading everyone's answers.

Lulu's favorite saying was "Painting is hell."

Taig's was "You have the right to remain silent."

On the page headed, "What do you think of the owner of this book," Rudy wrote, "A cool chick."

Lulu wrote, "A great sculptor."

Daphne wrote, "My best friend."

SATURDAY

"There she is!" cried Lara.

Stephanie drove down Park, turned, and came up.

Paula and Paul's doorman were waiting for them on the curb. They put Lara's things in the trunk.

"Good luck, sweethearts," Paula said. "Have a good semester. Drive carefully!"

"We'll miss her," the doorman said.

STEPHANIE'S EYES gleamed. "What's Daisy Summerfield like?"

"She's very funny."

"You'd never know it from her work."

"I know!"

"You'd have to be simple-minded to be that profound."

"But you couldn't understand her sculpture if you weren't sophisticated."

They exited the park, passed Daisy's building on West Eighty-Sixth Street without knowing it, turned right on West End Avenue, made a left on Ninety-Sixth, then another right, and they were northbound on the Henry Hudson Parkway.

The Best Art

1996

SATURDAY

"T he best art is anonymous," Daisy Summerfield said, turning
to look into the dark eyes of Alan Kodaly, at the entrance to
the gallery on Seventy-Ninth Street.

She was having a boss day.

"Buddhas, Gothic cathedrals, novels by A Lady, old Native
American baskets, African masks . . .

"No one should sign a work of art, because good art is a spiritual
expression.

"Stonehenge. Easter Island. Totem poles. People leave surprises for
each other."

Alan was relaxed and happy. He and Daphne had just come back
from France.

"Maybe I need a name change. Po Chü-i had a daughter, Summer
Dress." It made Daisy think of her old Lanz dresses. "I'd like the name
Summer Dress. You can call me Summer."

He held the door for Daisy, and gestured for her to follow him. Suddenly they were viewing one of her early sandstone sculptures.

It was like seeing an old photo of herself in a place she had forgotten. "Where did it come from?" she asked.

"Paris! The person who bought it returned it. Daphne wants to buy it. It's an odd piece," he apologized. "Not one of your signatures, not part of a series."

Candace, the Kodaly's society-girl receptionist, had called in sick, so they were alone. The sculpture stood on a white Formica pedestal and they walked around it.

At first it was like a familiar face that you can't place and then she recognized it.

It was a memory of Vermont's Pownal Valley in winter.

She had worked too hard on a row of scallops, broken one, and re-cut the whole thing lower down.

In anguish, she finished it hurriedly and asked Alan to get rid of it. "Daisy!"

Daphne and Daisy kissed, and Daisy examined her friend for new clothes or jewelry from Paris. Disappointingly, Daphne wore a familiar gray sweater and skirt.

"Sorry I couldn't have lunch with you and Alan. I missed you," she cried. Alan excused himself and went around the front desk to the door leading to the hall of offices.

"I missed you, too."

Daisy had a splinter of ice in her heart and had barely noticed her best friend's absence.

When she did, she saw it the way a painter regards an empty canvas.

Daphne had gone alone to every antiques store in Paris, looking for something for Daisy. "This is your birthday present," Daphne said, and handed Daisy a yellow ochre dragon.

"He's beautiful!" She counted his claws. There were five.

"Do you know what it is?"

"An Imperial Chinese dragon—and he's old!"

The Paris dealer said she had bought it in New York, where it was labeled "Bennington lion."

AFTER DAISY left by cab for the flea market downtown, Daphne walked around Daisy's sculpture from Paris.

"It's spiritual and joyful," she thought.

Daphne was thrilled to own it.

THE KODALY Gallery part-time porter always came to work through the back entrance.

Today he brought his fiancée, Francine, and her little son, Raymond, to see Brian Brighton's paintings.

They were going to eat at the Met. On the bus into Manhattan, Frankie said Daisy Summerfield had told him they could get vegetarian food there.

Brighton's paintings were small and at first they might think the artist was a child Raymond's age. But *The New York Times* printed long reviews of his work, and Candace had made copies of them.

They were on her desk. They could take one of each, and Raymond could take them to school.

Daphne had gone when Frankie arrived. The empty reception area was suddenly filled with Frankie's outrage.

"Go outside," he told Francine and Raymond. "Wait for me there. I'll show you this gallery another time."

Wearing his winter gloves, he hefted the very heavy sculpture and carried it to the mop room, where he set it behind the door and covered it with a clean rag.

It wasn't the first time Frankie had to remove an unsolicited artwork. Some artists couldn't believe that their work didn't interest the gallery.

"Believe it," he thought.

This was the first time an unknown sculptor had the effrontery to use one of their pedestals.

It was blasphemy.

The sculpture was a large stone with the word "GOD" in white letters.

Frankie stowed it away and went back to Francine and Raymond waiting outside. Then he hurried them west on Seventy-Ninth to see the big Christmas tree at the Met.

He apologized to God for working on the Sabbath and thanked Him for the chance to help Alan.

As Daisy was arriving at the Twenty-Sixth Street flea market; and Frankie, Francine, and Raymond were arriving at the Met; Alan greeted two couples in the Kodaly reception area.

Alan was sorry his clients missed Daisy but she would have had to comment on their name.

"Hello," Alan greeted them, "Mrs. Miaw, Mr. Miaw. I just had lunch with Daisy Summerfield."

"Really?"

They were thrilled! He caught the happy look Myra flashed at Gus Miaw.

Two years ago, Myra and Gus bought the smallest, least abstract, most charming Brian Brighton canvas.

It was also the least expensive, a mere $40,000.

"Shall we see the paintings?" Alan asked.

Brighton's work appealed to the child that adults no longer kept hidden. Like the town named for his family, his paintings were alive with resort colors.

"Such beautiful color," Mrs. Bateman said. She didn't mention how it would go with her decor. She had learned from Myra Miaw that talking about decor was gauche.

The Miaws liked *Cracking Walnuts with Walt*, and asked to see a price list.

Alan warned them that they'd never see another Brighton at the price they paid for theirs.

Mrs. Bateman went back to *A Small White Cape Amid White Capped Waves*.

Alan raised his eyebrows.

She shook her head, though her house was a white Cape, and her chintzes were turquoise, white, and beige.

"If we could afford it," she confided, "I would get a Daisy Summerfield sculpture."

"Really!"

"Yes, I'd love to have one of her stone sculptures to look at every day."

"None of her works is available now," he said smoothly. "Sometimes one comes up at auction."

"Then I bet a museum buys it," Mrs. Bateman said.

He felt flattered.

He went behind the reception desk and selected a few of Daisy's catalogs.

"With my compliments," he said, bowing.

After the Miaws and Batemans left, he caught up on work in his office.

IT WAS late in the day when a bad feeling about Daisy's old sculpture came over him.

He went out to the reception area.

The sculpture was gone.

The pedestal wasn't there, either.

He checked all the rooms and slowly came downstairs exhausted and unhappy.

SUNDAY

"Did you go to the flea market yesterday?"

Daisy was happy to hear from Alan so soon.

"Yes," she said. "I got something neat, and I got another neat thing today.

"One is a Palmer Cox Brownie figure and the other—you know Satsuma pottery, don't you? I never liked it. My grandparents had an umbrella stand that looked like it had a thousand cigar bands pasted on it.

"So today I got a vase I love. There's only a tiny bit of gold, so I know it wasn't made for export. That's why it was only sixty dollars. The dealer didn't know it was Satsuma."

Daisy chuckled.

"Daisy, I have something to tell you."

"What?"

"It's bad."

A museum was de-accessioning her sculpture. Her reputation was in an eclipse.

But did she really care, when she had two new pieces of china worthy of a scholarly paper about the twin islands, England and Japan?

She had washed the Palmer Cox Brownie and the vase, and studied them through her loupe.

Alan was describing his afternoon at the gallery, leading up to the bad thing.

"That's nice," Daisy said of Mrs. Bateman's remark.

The Brownie, wearing a yellow suit, was seated with his arms behind him.

"Stolen!" Daisy cried when Alan got to the point. "No, it must be in a storeroom or one of the offices."

"I looked."

"You didn't see it."

"I'll look again."

"You'll find it."

She tried not to mind his low opinion of her and hadn't noticed her sculpture was missing immediately even when a woman was telling him she loved her work.

"What did you think when you saw the empty pedestal?" she asked.

"It wasn't there."

"Then someone put it in a storeroom."

"Frankie wasn't there to move it. I have to report it."

"Who would you report it to?"

"My insurance company and the police."

"They won't find it! I don't want it in the papers. I would make me feel humiliated."

"Why?"

"Don't you feel gleeful when someone is robbed?"

"No!"

"Maybe it's a class thing."

"What do you mean?"

That he was rich and she was poor?

"I'll call Taig," he said without waiting for an answer.

"He'll do everything by the book!"

Alan was losing patience. "If I don't report it, my insurance is worthless."

"It's my piece."

"It's my gallery."

Daphne had been waiting downstairs.

She went up.

"Let's both think about it," he said, seeing Daphne frown. "And Daisy, I'm truly sorry."

"I'm guessing she doesn't want you to report it," Daphne said, as he put down the phone.

"No, and as she reminded me, it's her sculpture."

"I bought it! And it's your gallery."

"I said that. But it's her gallery, too."

Daphne looked incredulous.

"I wouldn't have a gallery without artists."

"It's my sculpture, and it's my gallery, too, for all the years I've worked there!"

She was so angry she burst into tears. Alan was her life, and that crackpot Daisy was her life.

"Stolen," thought Daisy.

She pictured a Mafia boss chewing on a cigar and gazing at the sculpture.

"God," he says, throwing down his stogie. "Get dat out 'a here!"

It makes him feel ashamed about his life of crime.

He has an idea. "Tie dat to Louie when youse drown 'im—after youse shoot 'im.

"Hey! Go get me some *scungilli*."

Having lightened the mood and placed her sculpture at Sheepshead Bay, she crawled to the back of her coat closet and started rocking a large stone onto a T-shirt.

She had two of these stones.

One at a time, she dragged them out.

Like the sculpture from Paris, they were larger than the stones she usually carved.

Now she had to get them on her stands.

She sat down on the floor and pulled one into her arms but couldn't get up.

She tried using her bed as leverage.

THERE HAD never been a theft at the gallery, and Alan was jet-lagged and not thinking clearly.

Daphne was jet-lagged and was upset.

Daisy was fine, but Alan didn't listen to her.

She had carved over a hundred sculptures in wood and stone, but he thought she was impractical and lacked common sense.

"MODESTO, CAN you help me? I have to put a heavy stone on a table."

He shut off the elevator and came in.

"Don't hurt yourself," she said, wringing her hands.

He put it on a stand and asked, "Do you want the other one on this table?"

"Can you do it?"

He put his finger to his lips.

And all these years she'd thought no one knew that she was carving in her apartment.

She saw him to the door and then celebrated, drinking cold coffee at her desk.

"SOUNDS LIKE you had a rough day," Taig said over the phone.

"Not really. Remember I said I found a Satsuma vase and I told you they made ugly pieces for export?"

She opened *Ceramics for the Collector* by George Savage.

"Listen to this."

> Japan has not received its due meed of praise for its keramic achievements. This is largely due to a misunderstanding. The Japanese too easily assumed that all Western peoples were cultural barbarians, and this led to the manufacture for export of the grossly over-decorated pottery of the 'Satsuma' type, although anything less like true Satsuma pottery it is difficult to conceive. The connoisseur of the West rather naturally assumed that these were products of the native Japanese taste, and quickly decided that the less he saw of them the better. However, prices were cheap, the stuff found a ready market in that section of the community whose natural taste had been killed by the mass-produced European wares of the nineteenth century, and the Japanese continued to turn it out. As a result, the Western and Japanese connoisseur have been at cross-purposes ever since.

"That's great," Taig said. "You're dealing with all this very well."

DAISY HAD taken out oils, turpentine, and a glass shelf from her medicine chest.

She squeezed out Lemon Yellow and Prussian Blue, selected a brush from her collection, dipped it in turpentine, then in blue, and painted the stone.

As she carved and painted, trying to find the stone's form, she built up patinas.

Daisy worked a little bristle brush into the yellow, and painted *Tu Fu* near the top.

She started leading her chisel sideways, making the stone slightly convex, making *Tu Fu* an inaccessible peak, and many thoughts went through her mind.

"You can't work like that! You should use power tools," her father said.

Her parents criticizing her hair and clothes.

They hated her ideas about the spirituality of art.

"I'm an empiricist," her mother said.

But after Mr. Summerfield died, her mother saw him in the living room.

"Morris?" she quavered.

Her mother called Daisy and said, "You're the only person I can tell."

MONDAY

While art galleries and museums took their Monday holiday, Daisy mixed Cadmium Red Light and Magenta, and painted the second stone.

She painted *Li Po* near the top in black.

She had nowhere to put her carving tools and brushes or her too-narrow palette.

She emptied her china cabinet, setting stacks on the floors of her closets. Then she walked the 6' x 16" x 32" pine cabinet to her front hall and squeezed past it.

Modesto said he could take it that night.

She was in love with her new work. "It's unbelievable," she kept saying.

DAISY NEEDED more room.

She rolled her desk chair to the service area outside in the hall.

It was gone by the time she took apart her Workbench desk and put it out there.

She called Con Ed, saying she smelled gas.

They came and disconnected her stove.

The super agreed to remove the stove, her refrigerator, and a wooden cabinet.

TUESDAY

"Remember, years ago, when Daisy gave a gallery talk?"

"What did she say?" Alan asked Daphne.

"The best thing God did was let people create. When you give money to a beggar, you should give enough so he can also give, because giving is a mitzvah. God made a mitzvah by giving us his gift so we can also create."

"I remember," Alan said.

Daphne put up her hair.

He said, "Maybe she'll find her sculpture at the flea market."

"I wouldn't tell her that!"

Silver-gilt light came through their bedroom window on Park Avenue.

Alan arranged the lengths of his navy-and-white silk tie against his starched white shirt.

When he left her dressing table mirror, Daphne saw a skein of hair standing away from her head.

She removed her combs, brushed her hair back and up, gathered it, twisted it, and held it as she picked up one comb and fastened it, then the other.

Following Alan downstairs, she asked, "Was it signed?"

Daphne hadn't seen a vertically connected *DS* that looked like a stick figure of a seahorse or a pennant flying from a badly bent pole inscribed near the bottom.

The doorman opened the street door and a blast of cold air hit them.

They pulled up their collars, lowered their heads, and walked over to the Camilla.

"I wish she'd marry Taig," Daphne said.

"What about her work?"

"What work? I think I'll have a cheese Danish. I haven't had one since I came to New York to see you every weekend."

"You said you were coming to work on your thesis."

"Do you remember the White Horse Tavern, Cafe Wha?, and the Fat Black Pussycat?"

"I thought, here's this cool college chick. I have to impress her."

"Sitting with Franz Kline at the Cedar Bar was very impressive."

"Good," Alan said.

"Do you remember eating at Rikers and the Chuck Wagon at four in the morning?"

"I do."

"Remembrance has a rear and front—/'Tis something like a house." Daphne quoted Emily Dickinson.

"Are you enjoying the pastry?"

"Very much."

ALAN AND Daphne arrived at the gallery. Alan asked Melanie and Vincent to come to his office.

He told them about the robbery, then closed his door and called his lawyer.

"I want to make my wife a director and vice president," he said. "It's long overdue."

"You don't have to. She's your heir."

Alan said, "Wait, make her a full partner."

Mary Ann at his insurance company told him to send her a copy of the bill of sale and she'd take care of it.

He forgot to ask if he should report it to the police. Common sense said, make the call.

The officer who answered the phone wanted to know where the gallery was located.

After almost a hundred years in his building, Alan would have thought they'd know.

"Any sign of a break-in?"

"I told you it happened around lunchtime when the gallery was open."

"So anyone could have walked off wid it."

"It's a two-foot-high piece of sandstone. It weighs well over a hundred pounds!"

"Any identifying marks?"

"Do you have an art expert I can speak to?"

"You're reporting a robbery."

"It's an art robbery."

"Any identifying marks?"

"It's two feet tall and wedge shape."

"Wedge shape?"

"If you stand a slice of pie on its crust, that's the shape."

"A pie stands on the crust. That's what the crust is for."

"I mean the back that's crimped," Alan said impatiently. "In other words, it's an isosceles triangle that rests on its base. One side is blue and says 'God' in white letters. The other has multiple cuts representing trees and is dark red.

"It's a gorgeous piece. I'll go into more detail when you send someone over."

"Over where? You know where it is?"

"Thank you for your help."

He walked into the gallery and heard Candace on the phone gossiping about the robbery.

FRANKIE ARSENEAULT got a phone call from the porter at James Rose Antique China. Not for the first time, Frankie wished he was at the Kodaly every day to be there for Alan and Daphne.

FRANKIE TOLD Francine that a sculpture of Daisy's was stolen.

"NO!" she bellowed.

They loved Daisy.

He said it had a label from a Paris gallery, and that would help identify it.

"What about the one you put in the mop room?"

"Daisy wouldn't do that."

"It's not a blaspheme!"

But he thought the devil made it, because even when he held Francine's substantial body after Raymond had gone to bed, his arms felt empty.

TAIG HAD finished testifying before a grand jury and come uptown to see Daisy.

She covered her sculptures with sheets and opened the door, looking just the same as usual.

"Try not to walk on the chips," she said. "It'll scratch the floor."

Chips?

Whoa. He stepped on one.

"Now you have paint on your shoe. Don't walk on it."

"What's going on?"

"I'm working."

"Really? Just like that?"

"Don't talk and jinx me." Her grandparents had given her a tremendous fear of *kinehora*.

"See you for dinner tomorrow?"

"Sure," he said, backing out the door.

Daisy went deep into carving a representation of a sheer mountain that to her was the embodiment of a 1,300-year-old poet.

Taig didn't mention the call from Alan Kodaly and the request that Taig stop by the gallery. He had only a passing knowledge about the *kinehora* from Daisy. It never came up in Horsefly. Taig thought it best to play it safe and stay silent.

DAISY CALLED the Sculpture Shop.

"Elsie, hi, this is Daisy Summerfield."

"Hi," Elsie said, unimpressed.

"I was going to come there after the flea market, but I didn't go. Do you have one or two pieces of sandstone you can send me?"

Elsie came out of her lethargy. "We can't choose a stone for you!"

"If it's sandstone and about two feet tall, I'll take it."

"Can we send a piece of sandstone uptown to Daisy Summerfield?" Elsie asked Bruce.

"No."

"Tell him I'll buy a sculpture stand, too," Daisy pleaded, putting on her boots.

SHE PAID for a piece of sandstone and a stone-carvers stand, and went out to find a taxi.

A driver stopped but refused to wait. He would have left anyway, when he saw her purchases.

"You couldn't have chosen a worse time of day," Bruce said, laughing. "You'll have to leave them."

"I can't! I just started carving again!"

She had been buying materials from him since she was nineteen, and had always liked him.

Bruce locked up and put her things in his truck.

As they rode up Tenth Avenue, she learned that he was married and had grandchildren.

"I don't believe it!"

"Where does the time go?" he asked.

He parked in front of the hydrant and took the things to her vestibule.

She unlocked the lobby door and was pushing down the stop to keep it open as he drove away.

First she set the stand near the elevator.

Then she rolled the stone on to the doormat and dragged it into the lobby.

She had to go down to the basement, find the porter, and ask him to bring up a hand truck.

He wheeled the stone into her apartment and placed it on the stand.

She cleaned it, painted it pink, and printed "Wang Wei" near the top in black.

Her phone rang.

"Guess who's a director of the gallery," Daphne said.

"Melanie."

"No, I am!"

"I know you are."

"Did Alan tell you he was making me a director and full partner?"

"You mean you weren't?"

"No."

"Well, he finally did the right thing."

She couldn't tell Daphne she was working, because Daphne would tell Alan and it was too soon. Rothko said people could impair his paintings by looking at them.

WEDNESDAY

"Even if there's no way the sculpture can possibly be there, we look," Taig said.

Melanie and Vincent made up his team of three. He believed in Daisy's hunch that it was still somewhere in the building.

Melanie emerged from the third office closet pairing a stack of wool gloves.

"Aren't these pretty? I think they were Pamela's. Do I have to find her and return them?"

"No," said the rugged law enforcement officer. "You should keep them."

They entered the fourth office.

"Nothing here," Vincent said, and they moved on to the fifth office.

Taig was bored. The little world of the gallery was airless and humdrum.

He had a thought that might engage Daisy: all art is used, second-hand, past its expiration date the minute it leaves the sculpture stand or easel.

Then the threesome carefully examined the packing and shipping areas.

Last, they entered the mop room and found it.

"WHAT DO you think?" cried Daisy over the phone.

"I'm sure it was a mistake," said Taig.

Too late, Taig realized she meant what he thought of the sculpture. He told her the story.

"Now it's on its way to Daphne and Alan's," he concluded.

"Wait! Tell them to hold off," Daisy said. "I want it for my show. I need you to bring it here. Only Alan doesn't know I'm working, and I don't want to tell him yet, so just think of something."

ON THE way up Broadway to Mana, Daisy's new favorite restaurant, where each macrobiotic dish was freshly prepared, Taig put forward his new theory about art being secondhand.

Daisy waved him off.

Her attitude was that art gave her a feeling for the universe—open, intelligent, and respectful.

She viewed art and philosophy joined, as a sky full of stars.

While they waited for a table, they watched the diners chew slowly, deliberating what to pick up next with their chopsticks.

"How can people think they know God? It's a concept!" Daisy said.

She thought, "What is life but stories?"

Stories she told herself while carving. Stories shared with wood and stone.

Stories of her life.

Stories she heard when her head touched her pillow.

Stories she read.

Maggie Tulliver saying, "I'll have that with the jam run out."

"The fellow who hid your sculpture meant well," he said. "His religion may not be for everyone, but I think he's a good man."

"I do, too."

"You know, I was thinking about the sculpture," Taig began, "it's transcendental—"

"I know! Isn't it a great use of sandstone?"

Taig looked at her and thought, "I'll never get it right."

SATURDAY

"Going to the flea market?" he asked. Lately on weekend mornings, after eating at the coffee shop, Taig and Daisy rode downtown together.

She got off at Twenty-Eighth, and he stayed on the train until Park Place, then walked to One Police Plaza.

Today she said, "I'm going to the Sculpture Shop. Come with me and meet Bruce and Tom."

Shocked at the sudden invitation to be part of Daisy's world, he went along.

Daisy introduced Taig to Bruce and Tom who had cleared a path to the sandstone.

She said, "I'll take all four stones."

She made her way back to Bruce. "I need another stand. Mine wobble."

"That's not good!"

"Do you remember the mahogany stands I bought in 1960?"

"I told you they were for display! I bought them to help an old sculptor who needed money." He laughed. "I bet that's why you stopped carving."

The Big Show

1998

FRIDAY

Melanie's phone was blinking.

"What's NFS?" asked a man by the desk.

"It means it's not for sale. We borrowed it from a collector to complete the exhibit."

The fax machine beeped.

> *Sold!*
> *We're delighted to buy* Mrs. Todd in a Boat
> *and bring a little New England to L.A.*
> *The Getty Museum*

"So what is for sale?" the man asked.

"Only the works of other artists, I'm sorry," Melanie said, adding the Getty's dot to number 10, a delicately painted limestone boulder.

- • 1. *Red Li Po*, oil paint on sandstone, 1996 (300,000)
- • 2. *Yellow Li Po*, oil paint on sandstone, 1996 (300,000)

- 3. *White Wang Wei*, oil paint on sandstone, 1996 (300,000)
- 4. *Pink Wang Wei*, oil paint on sandstone, 1996 (300,000)
- 5. *Black Tu Fu*, oil paint on sandstone, 1997 (300,000)
- 6. *Blue Tu Fu*, oil paint on sandstone, 1997 (300,000)

NFS 7. *Witness: Black River*, granite, 1978

- 8. *Witness: Royal Pavilion Hospital*, granite, 1984 & 1998 (175,000)

NFS 9. *Mrs. Todd*, oil sticks on limestone, 1979 & 1998

- 10. *Mrs. Todd in a Boat*, oil sticks on limestone, 1998 (350,000)
- 11. *Mrs. Todd and Her Mother*, oil paint on sandstone, 1998 (350,000)
- 12. *Landscapes*, oil paint on sandstone, 1997 (300,000)
- 13–16. *Four Tombs: "Blue," "Bird," "Of," "Happiness,"* recycled brownstone and Plexiglas, 1997 (1,000,000)

DAISY'S STUDIO was clean and empty. She couldn't remember doing the work now on exhibit.

Except for the one Daphne and Alan owned, she would never see those sculptures again.

In her mind, she could envision more in the Mrs. Todd series: *Mrs. Todd in the Herb Plot* and *Mrs. Todd and "The Queen's Twin,"* but that work was done now. She had learned at an early age not to repeat past successes.

HARRIETTA TAIG would have been happy if Daisy repeated herself at least once more. She wanted a limestone Mrs. Todd, but her husband delayed on the last one for a day, and now it was sold.

He felt like killing himself when Harrietta told him Sarah Orne Jewett's Mrs. Todd was her idol.

Harrietta was one of the few people who could tell you that.

If Mrs. Todd had occasion to step into the far corner of her herb plot, she trod heavily upon thyme, and made its fragrant presence known with all the rest. Being a very large person, her full skirts brushed and bent almost every slender stalk that her feet missed.

Harrietta wanted to enjoy it and leave it to Daisy in her will.

Henry wasn't fond of Daisy, even less so now. He thought she was a charming star, cold and aloof.

DAISY'S PHONE rang.

"Hi, Daisy! I just wanted to apologize again that your new catalog isn't what we discussed," Melanie said. "I should have told you before."

Melanie had written the catalog for Daisy's sold-out show and thought of the title "Daisy Summerfield: Chinese and American Landscapes."

Daisy wasn't much help to Melanie in the writing. Daisy knew nothing about her art but would admire it if she came upon it unaware.

Daisy didn't want Melanie to know that she was disappointed. She wanted to read about the crimes she had solved, but ideas fluttered and fell.

"I have enough material for a monograph," Melanie said, and Daisy hoped again.

DAISY WAS rereading her catalog when Taig came in.

She read her reviews forty, eighty, a hundred times, like "someone of the past," as the poet says in *The Tale of Genji*.

"Want to go out for soba noodles?" Taig asked.

Despite the astronomical selling prices at the show, Daisy still needed cheering up. First, there was the gallery's cut, then taxes.

In a meeting that went from giddily happy to depressing, Daisy's tax accountant pointed out that she'd had no real income for fourteen years. The money she was getting from the show was less per year than a junior office manager took home.

The accountant knew this because her nephew was a junior office manager in Manhattan.

On top of all that, the accountant said, Daisy couldn't be sure when she'd work again. So the money might have to last a long time.

"Don't spend any of it," the accountant counseled.

A few months later, Daisy was told the accountant had died from a leak in her chimney that she never had repaired.

THURSDAY

"Do you have a minute?"

Daphne looked up.

"I told Daisy I'd write about the crimes she solved," Melanie said, "but this catalog wasn't appropriate for that."

"No, of course not. You did a great job."

"Thanks. It wrote itself."

"Oh, I don't know. When did you speak to her about doing a catalog?"

"When you were in the hospital, and we were so worried about you."

Melanie found it hard to believe this elegant woman had been coshed.

"It was interesting to write about her turning your *God* sculpture into a Mrs. Todd."

Melanie wondered how Daphne felt about it.

Daisy wrote "DAPHNE + ALAN" on a photo of the re-carved piece.

"She just made a fortune," Daphne said. "Maybe I should sue her. But no. The gallery did very well, too."

"I think I understand her," her old friend said. "I'd say her agenda is to use her gifts down to the nub to show her appreciation for them, and die with a pure soul and a light heart."

Standing in her office, Melanie felt a greater respect for Daphne than any of their artists.

"May I have Daisy's china photographed for a monograph on her?" she asked.

"Go for it," Daphne said.

"I GOT rid of it," Daisy told Melanie on the phone.

"She got rid of it," Melanie told Arlene, her partner.

"What! The china you wanted to write about? What did she do with it?"

"She probably smashed it."

"Lefty!"

That was her nickname for Melanie Lefkowitz.

"It's just that the greed and violence might have made it successful. I even had a title: *The Crimes of Daisy Summerfield.*"

Arlene gave Melanie's shoulder a sympathetic squeeze.

An Evening Skirt

1999

TUESDAY

"The bluebird tombs will look terrific," Daphne said.

"I was a Bluebird," Daisy said. "Then I flew up to Camp Fire Girl. I think I went higher. Horizon Girl?"

"How people love to talk," thought Daphne. "I remember when you bought the bluebirds."

"I bought them from Mr. Flea. Thanks for reminding me! I still need to give him an invitation."

She forgot the invitations every weekend.

Opening night of the show at the Metropolitan Museum was just a week away.

WEDNESDAY

"Hi, Daphne."

"Quick question. Melanie wants to know if you have a special cleaner for the *Tombs*."

"Uh, no."

"We'll use the one we always use on Plexiglas. What are you wearing to the opening?" Daphne asked.

"Jeans, a shirt, and the pearl necklace you and Alan gave me."

"We want to buy you a gown."

"Let's go to Comme des Garçons."

"We'll go to Bloomingdale's and get something that has presence, so you don't have to work."

Surprised by Daphne's insight, she agreed to meet her at 11:00 on Friday.

"Meet me on the ground floor, Lexington Avenue side, in front of the stairs. If you want to look at socks or hair clips, go early."

TAIG SAT down next to a paperback on the couch, *Blonde Like Me*.

"Going to dye your hair?"

"I've been blond all my life!"

"Really?"

Her heart sank. "How can you not know my hair color?"

"You don't have a hair color."

"It's faded."

"I'm sorry."

"I'm an ash blond, a 'Moon blonde,' the least dangerous of the most lethal type," she said, picking up the book.

"'Moon blondes fire unquenchable longing,'" she read aloud. "'They are interested in conquering but have no desire to colonize.'"

She stopped, embarrassed.

FRIDAY

Escalator up!
  "I always lose my identity here. I can't find myself in the mirror," Daisy said.

Immediately, among the Steinbergian busts of women, she saw her own pale face.

"I don't know how you could mistake yourself," Daphne turned and said.

"I used to like Saint Laurent."

They arrived on the designer floor.

"You wore nothing but Yves Saint Laurent Rive Gauche for years," Daphne thought.

There was the department ahead of them—and there was the skirt.

"We're getting a gown," Daphne said.

The skirt was beautiful.

"What would you wear on top?" she asked on the way to the dressing room.

The saleswoman said she'd bring some tops.

Daisy planned to wear it with one of her plaid flannel shirts and work boots.

Modeling it, she was so pleased she said so.

The saleswoman cried, "Don't you dare!"

Daphne wanted to shout, "Artists set the styles you slavishly follow!"

If Oscar de la Renta had been there, he might have snipped off Daisy's collar and added a *tulle fichu*.

The saleswoman wanted to call in a fitter.

Daisy didn't care for a fitter's opinion.

She supervised the packing and then looked at costume jewelry.

"DID YOU get her a gown?" Alan asked.

"An evening skirt," Daphne replied.

"What will she wear on top?"

"She has a top."

"Make her show it to you."

"I can't."

"What does the skirt look like?"

"It's black velvet, very full, over an *écru* net crinoline."

"Sounds good!"

LINDA LEONE stopped by Daisy's apartment and she modeled her new outfit.

Linda squealed, "You look like a cute little woodsman ballerina!"

Daisy had rolled the waistband twice to make the proportions work with her boots.

"I had a great idea!" Linda said.

"What?"

"I'm going to make lithos of Myron's sculptures!"

"That is great."

"Can I do your sculpture, too?"

"Of course."

SATURDAY

"Oh-h-h-h-h-h-h-h-h, no!"

The invitation frightened Mr. Flea.

"Do you remember the plastic bluebirds I bought?"

"Gimme twenty-eight dollars."

"What?" But he was giving a price for a turquoise-and-black vase, and when the man who was looking at it left, she bought it.

Daisy had given Mr. Flea all her china when she started working and needed the space. Over time, the discounts he gave became smaller until she stopped bringing it up.

Daisy wasn't sure Mr. Flea would know what to do with most valuable pieces but was leaving that to him and to the gods of the flea market. She felt like a fisherman, returning a beautiful catch back into the sea.

"Do you remember the plastic bluebirds I bought?" she said again. "The invitation is for a show that includes them."

"What bluebirds?" he asked, clearly at a loss.

DAISY STAYED at the flea market chatting with everyone she knew, complaining about her *Four Tombs* going to the Met, and carrying on about her old Cinderella watch. It had come in a clear plastic slipper and inspired the tombs.

"Everyone here is looking for something," Rich Bingham said, and they laughed.

"You know, the flea market's closing," Mr. Flea said.

"They've been saying that for years." Daisy was not taking the bait.

"Well, it's happening."

THE TURQUOISE-AND-BLACK vase from Mr. Flea looked identical to one described in *Pottery and Porcelain* ("*Rakka 11th to 12th cent.*") this way:

> They have the blazing of hot skies and ominous sunsets as well as the blue black cobalt of nights with stars too many and too large.

SUNDAY

Daisy looked at a bowl with variegated green glaze that formed a dark pool inside it.

Six months ago, the dealer called the bowl early American and wanted fifty dollars for it.

"How much is it?" Daisy asked.

"Thirty."

"I'll take it."

"I'm holding it for someone. He went to the bank for the money."

"How about I just take it and go?"

Daisy paid.

While handing it to her, the dealer shouted, "She just bought the bowl you wanted!"

Daisy glimpsed a small brassy-haired man as she fled down the aisle with her purchase.

"Miss Summerfield!" said a stocky, dark-eyed man. He was at a table of cuckoo clocks and held one lovingly in his hands. "You don't remember me."

"Yes I do. Mike Angeli!"

"Have you solved any more crimes?" he asked. "I still never solved one."

"That can't be true!"

"You were right to choose Taig instead of me."

"I didn't choose him."

"Are you still with him?"

"Yes, seven years."

"Congratulations."

She said, "You're a good detective! You gather information. The crimes get solved."

"Some," he admitted.

She had an invitation to the show at the Met in her pocket. She gave it to him and that made him very happy.

"Buy you a cup of coffee," she said.

"Sure!"

She started toward the exit and the Fritzie Coffee Shop near her subway on Seventh Avenue.

"Let's go uptown." She wanted to treat him to something nice.

He wished his fellow officers could see him with her and hear her speak.

"How's Mrs. Kodaly?" he asked.

"Fine."

She pranced a little and smiled up at him, thinking, "This is what I need."

The precision of flirting while seeming to do the opposite exhausted her.

"I'd better eat," she said, turning at Forty-Fourth.

They entered a Japanese restaurant. She had plenty of cash, and she had invited him.

At first, the crisp salad and hot green tea made her feel better.

Then she felt worse.

As she chatted in a thin voice, she noticed a small brassy-haired man at the sushi bar. Was he the man she fled from at the flea market? But there was something else.

The man was someone she feared. She racked her brain for a reason.

Could she have had a mini-stroke? She set down her cup and put her hands to her face. It felt normal, and when she spoke her mouth didn't drag.

"I don't feel well."

They were at a table in a back corner.

Mike went to the restroom and called Taig, then paid the bill and put her in a cab.

SHE WAS surprised to see Taig at the curb.

"You okay?" he asked.

She had napped coming home through the park.

Before Mike's call, Taig heard from his two operatives that John Lorimer was at a sushi bar on East Forty-Fifth Street.

As Mike and Daisy left, the first operative lurched into Lorimer and spilled his saki.

Taig and Daisy rode upstairs.

She lay on the bed as he stood over her.

"Daisy," Taig said, "you need to be careful."

"Why?" she asked.

"John Lorimer is back in town. You may not recognize him. He lost weight and bleached his hair."

He handed Daisy a photograph.

Daisy didn't say "He's cute" as she had the last time she was given his photograph.

"This is the man I saw! It was him at the flea market and the sushi restaurant!"

"I know. I hired retired detectives to shadow you, keep you safe. Just until we know for sure."

"WHAT?"

"If there's any chance he could harm you—"

"Any chance? He already tried once! You were the one who thought his knife was a work of art and let him go!"

Daisy's anger and bitterness shocked her, but she trusted it.

"Is it too much to expect you to believe me?!" Daisy shouted.

"I barely knew you then—" Taig began.

"I don't need you to protect me!"

"I don't need this," Taig said tightly and went for the door. "I'm going to Chelsea."

And he left, as mad at her as she was at him. But he didn't go to Chelsea. He joined the surveillance team keeping an eye on Daisy's apartment.

TUESDAY

"You're the most wonderful driver," Daisy said, halfway through the park.

"I wish I knew more about art. Your sculpture must be outstanding."

"Same level as your driving. You know what they say, 'If you can draw you can drive.'"

"I hadn't heard that."

"Did you ever try drawing?"

"No."

Daisy was in a great mood. As she was leaving, she saw her hair was drying well.

He parked in a space in front of the museum. Daisy started to open her door. He asked her to wait until he came around and opened it.

She walked up the steps and Joe De Leo gave her a very warm hug.

As they entered the Great Hall, she said, "I'm so glad to be exhibiting with two people I like."

They went up to the mezzanine. Across the expanse of the Great Hall below them, in the place where the Rodins were exhibited forty years ago, a giant sign read "Three Contemporary Sculptors at the Close of the Century."

The cup of a giant funnel lay on its side. Joe De Leo's work.

"Have you seen mine?" she asked, pointing to a line of four dark stones pierced with light.

They seemed placed the way she specified. The plastic bluebirds were inside them. Whatever Melanie used to clean the piece, it did gleam.

He was embarrassed. "I saw your show three times. The Kodalys must have told you it sold out. Who knew when I was so excited about Taig being my patron, you'd be with his son? How come you aren't married?"

"We're, I guess you could say, not together right now."

"Too bad. Though maybe that means I still have a shot? C'mon, don't you want to be with someone who understands you?"

"I doubt I could stand the excitement."

THE THIRD artist in the exhibition was Myron Kantrowitz.

For forty years, Myron had soldered and welded what Daisy called junk balls. Now his work was simply magnificent.

As Joe went to get a drink, Daisy scanned the crowd for Myron.

"Have you seen Daphne and Alan?" she asked Lulu King.

Lulu looked like a gold *lamé* mountain.

"Where is Mr. Flea, darling? I've been looking everywhere!"

They strolled past the glass cases of Asian ceramics to get to the new exhibit.

"Look at you!" Lulu cried, kissing Joe as he came back with drinks. "You look so handsome in a tuxedo."

"Have my drink, Lulu," Daisy said. She hoped to get a closer look at Myron's sculpture.

Daisy felt a hand on her arm.

"Excuse me. Hi, Daisy Summerfield? Do you remember me? I'm Chris. We met at the Kodaly anniversary *soirée*."

DAPHNE DUCKED behind the temporary wall of the exhibit to check the clasp on her pearls.

"Hello," said Lorimer.

She blushed.

"How was Australia?" she asked, trying not to smile at his brassy blond hair.

"I rue the day we spoke about Daisy Summerfield doing my portrait."

He debated whether to take her pearls, decided not to, and went back to the party.

None of his plans for the evening included killing Daphne.

He took a *canapé*.

This was his home, filled with ancestral armor, statuary, furniture, china, silver, paintings, and fabrics.

He used to love coming down the stairs to the Great Hall, nodding at the guards.

He took another *canapé* and tasted it critically. "Excellent," he thought.

Summerfield cheated him out of his birthright. He left because of her.

Lorimer felt the knife in his pocket, put his thumb on the button, and moved toward her.

IT WAS the height of the evening. The well-heeled crowd was thick and noisy.

It could happen any minute now.

Daisy, waving her hands and waggling her fingers, was talking to Chris Ryan.

Lorimer fixed his eyes on her.

He would have liked her to die pleading with him, but he knew he couldn't have everything.

"Small world," Chris was saying.

"Not really. I'm one of the sculptors."

He had aged since they met at the Kodaly party. He had gray hair and a little pot belly.

"Do you teach literature?"

"No, I write murder mysteries about an old comic character called Mopsy."

She cried, "OH MY GOD! YOU'RE GLADYS PARKER!!"

Daisy felt someone behind her and stepped aside as Chris sank to his knees.

She thought he was thanking her for liking his books.

Then she saw Taig step around him.

Taig grabbed Lorimer and held him but Chris had already been stabbed through the heart.

DAPHNE AND Alan took Daisy to their apartment. She was still in shock and needed her friends.

"It's over now, at least," Alan said.

"And Taig was right there," Daphne said. "Whatever has happened, he must still love you."

Daisy started to cry.

"Chris Ryan was Gladys Parker! He wrote the *Mopsy* books!" Daisy wailed.

"He still shouldn't have been killed," Daphne said.

THURSDAY

It was the night of Myron Kantrowitz's biggest solo show in years and Daisy wouldn't have missed it.

Wearing work boots and a black-watch plaid flannel shirt over her black velvet skirt, she stepped out of a cab on Greene Street.

Lights blazed in a small brick building.

Old-fashioned black-and-gold letters on the window spelled "Kantrowitz & Son."

Myron greeted her at the door, and she looked up and saw the shot that would be in the *Times*.

The review would say that his father put up the money to fabricate his indoor steel sculpture.

"It's brilliant!" she cried.

"THEY ARE articulated paintings," she thought, pacing among the girders.

Myron had translated Franz Kline back into steel.

"Thanks to him," she thought, "we can live with this art and hang our clothes and holiday lights on it."

Rudy Shayne wanted to know what Daisy thought of the sculpture.

"It synthesizes the art of the twentieth century."

"Shit," he said.

Daisy went to Myron, her face pale and earnest.

"I'm so proud to know you. God bless you," she croaked.

"C'mere," he said. "I want you to meet someone."

Jon Cohn, one of Myron's many friends, had come to the party early.

"Tell Jon about the crimes you solved."

"Crimes?" asked Jon. "By the way, I'm not just a fan. I own two of your pieces."

"I hate amateur detectives who get people killed. I had a perfect record until Tuesday night."

"Good grief."

Jon was medium height and a little overweight.

Daisy liked his girth and what she took to be kindness in his gray eyes. "Maybe this is who I should be with," she thought.

His tux was as old and spotted as Myron's was new and rented.

"What do you do?" she asked.

"I'm in a think tank."

She clasped her hands. "Where?"

"Seattle."

She had always wanted to live there.

JOE DE Leo held her to him, compulsively kissing her hair, knowing that Lorimer tried to kill her.

Everyone tried to crash Myron's opening. The police had to cordon off the area.

Daisy greeted Daphne as a roar went up. "What was that?"

A pretty movie star kissed Myron.

"I'm so grateful to be part of the New York art world," Daisy said to Daphne, tears in her eyes. "You didn't say anything about my skirt!"

"You look the same as the other night."

"That's good, isn't it?"

"Of course," Daphne said.

Daisy had brought a little bag of roasted chestnuts. She didn't need to, the food was wonderful. She had two tofu dogs with sauerkraut and two steamed bean balls.

JON COHN reappeared and invited Daisy to a party the following night.

"I'd love to," she said, sounding like one of the little women in *Little Women*, "but this is my only gown."

"READY TO go?" asked Alan.

"Can we drop you off?" he asked Daisy.

"No, I think I'll go with one of Myron's friends."

As the night went on, there was a wall of flowers outside the Kantrowitz building. Young artists coming from neighborhood bars were paying tribute to Myron.

Daisy left with Jon Cohn, giving him ideas for the think tank:

- Lightweight, long-lasting batteries. Could felt be used?
- Books we own, but never read, speak to us from our shelves.

- A DNA controlled laser vacuum to pick up dictators anywhere in the world.
- Learn to develop pictures taken by the earth's atmosphere.

He was planning to be with Daisy all the way until breakfast.

OUTSIDE, PAST the flowers, there was Taig.

"Hi," Daisy said.

"Interested in talking?" he asked.

Daisy stood between the two men and opened her bag of roasted chestnuts.

Farewell, Mr. Flea

2000

MONDAY

The accident happened on Route 35 in Horsefly.

Henry Taig Sr., eighty-six, had a massive stroke at a red light.

Harrietta, eighty-one, pulled the emergency brake, turned on the emergency lights, and punched 911 on her cell phone.

She felt for his pulse, didn't find it, and opened her door and got out, hoping to flag down a doctor.

A young TV anchor, speeding while talking on his cell phone, killed her.

Daisy thought it was a miracle. She believed our death dates are engraved on our hearts.

The Taigs never contradicted each other. They left the earth together.

Neither of them had a health problem, and suddenly they were gone.

WHEN TAIG learned about his parents' deaths, he called Daisy.

She went downstairs and waited for him at her corner.

From the West Side Highway to the Henry Hudson Parkway to the Saw Mill Parkway, to 117, he talked about securing the house.

They turned on to Route 35 and saw his father's car.

"You can't stop here," an officer said, as Taig got out.

"I'm Henry Taig Jr. You have my parents' keys."

The officer embraced him.

"Do you know him from high school?" asked Daisy, when he handed her the keys.

"I've never seen him before."

A large glass cube overhung by a cedar roof appeared at the top of a hill.

Ancient Oriental carpets strewn on the Buffalo grass were actually brick artwork by Margaret Kerr.

Taig circled the house on the gravel driveway, stopped, and he and Daisy got out.

He opened a door concealed in the glass arcade surrounding the stone building, unlocked a sliding steel door, and they entered the living room.

Daisy stayed near the door as Taig checked the locks in the kitchen and two bedrooms.

He locked the glass door as he left.

Daisy walked through the arcade. On the south or kitchen side stood palm trees in huge ceramic pots.

The east side consisted of two bedrooms separated by enormous closets. The southeast was the master bedroom. The northeast bedroom was Taig's. He and Daisy had shared that room when they made rare visits. The north side also contained the seed within the core—the utility room.

The floor throughout the arcade and interior was a rough blue-green tile. On it were sisal rugs, and classic furniture by George Nelson, Le Corbusier, Mies van der Rohe, and Arne Jacobsen.

The living and dining area displayed two Pollocks and two Newmans. Grace Hartigan's *The Kitchen Sink* was in the kitchen along with two platters painted by Picasso in the town of Vallauris. A Joan Mitchell diptych hung in the master bedroom. Taig's old bedroom had a Guston. Many more artworks were crated in storage. Daisy found her two sculptures in one of the closets with a Bonnard.

She turned the corner and was back on the west side to watch the sunset.

Taig returned from seeing his mother and father at the morgue.

Daisy went into a bathroom, overcome with emotion.

When she came out, her sculptures were back on the console with the González.

That was when he begged Daisy to marry him and offered her the house.

DAPHNE ANSWERED her phone.

"Where are you?" she asked Daisy. "Did you forget we were having lunch?"

"I'm in Horsefly. Taig's parents were killed in a car crash."

"WHAT?"

This was big news for the art world, and Daphne was the first to hear it.

"I'll be there in the morning with Vincent. You need a registrar for the artwork. Alan's in California. Please give Taig my love and sympathy."

"Oh, and we're getting married," Daisy said casually.

"WHEN?"

"I don't know."

"Put Taig on the phone!"

"You should strike while the iron is hot!" Daphne told him, knowing Daisy. "Let's shoot for Sunday."

TUESDAY

No one wanted to open the Taigs' cupboards or refrigerator.

Daisy and Taig had paper cups of coffee, when Daphne and Vincent arrived.

While everyone inventoried artwork, Daphne drove into town. Several of the gallery's clients had homes in Horsefly, and she knew her way around.

Her first stop was the restaurant, the Blue Dragon. It was once a Chinese restaurant but was now Italian. Alfredo, the owner, liked the name and kept it.

Alfredo agreed to open Sunday, a day the restaurant was always closed, for the wedding ceremony and reception.

The menu included polenta with large grilled shrimp, plates of fresh tomatoes, avocado, mixed greens, bread, olives, figs chilled and quartered, biscotti, and espresso.

Alan would buy champagne, and she would order a cake at the Baker's Cafe.

Dᴀᴘʜɴᴇ ʟᴏᴏᴋᴇᴅ in store windows as she walked up Main Street.

She came to a florist.

"I would have forgotten flowers," she thought.

Aᴛ ᴛʜᴇ Baker's Cafe, Cheryl, a small woman with curly blond hair, came out of the kitchen to speak to her.

They discussed nondairy substitutes, but Cheryl said she had never used them, so Daphne thought, "Oh, what the heck, Daisy's not pure vegan," and ordered strawberry shortcake made with whipped cream.

Oɴ Bᴇᴅꜰᴏʀᴅ Road, Daphne stopped at a stop sign and saw a thrift shop she'd never noticed. "Daisy will like that," she thought.

Daphne took a sharp right when she saw a bridal shop.

Looking around the shop as if she were Daisy, she found a pink nylon veil attached to a headband.

Back at the Taigs', she handed the sack to Daisy.

"It's a headpiece," she said. "You don't have to wear it."

But Daisy loved herself in it.

THURSDAY

The Taigs had been cremated.

Daisy wanted to put their ashes in the clear stream on their property.

They met with an old friend of Henry Sr.'s, Judge Nawi, to sign papers.

"Would they like that?" she asked the judge.

"Who?"

"The Taigs."

"The DEP won't allow it."

"HOW COULD your parents like him?" she asked Taig later.

She loved the idea of putting their ashes under a willow by the clear water that ran through their property.

Her property now.

When Taig proposed, he said, "I'll sweeten the deal. I'll sell you the house for a dollar."

Daisy accepted, and it was her land, her roof over them, as they sat on her furniture.

It pained her to open her wallet in the law office and give him a dollar.

But back on the street before parting, he gave her a twenty.

SUNDAY

Near the cash register in the center of the diner, Judge Nawi married Taig and Daisy.

Snapdragons, daisies, and other garden flowers were in glass vases on the tables. Daphne put one vase next to the cash register.

Taig surprised Daisy with his signet ring. She surprised him by crying tears of joy.

VINCENT SAID, "I wanted to dance with the bride."

"Everyone talks to the bride instead." Daisy flung back the veil, as though it were hair.

In her glasses, short-sleeve plaid shirt, jeans, and moccasins, she looked very amusing.

"Thanks so much for getting the artwork into storage."

"My pleasure."

"You spent a day in Queens!"

"No problem."

"Everything's there?"

"Except your two sculptures and the Burchfield."

She looked for Taig and saw him sitting in a booth, talking to the judge and his wife, Trudy.

"THAT WAS a totally glamorous wedding. Be happy." Melanie kissed her.

For someone who didn't like getting kissed, Daisy was getting kissed a lot.

She inhaled Trudy Nawi's face powder and choked.

"It was like something from *Harper's Bazaar* in the seventies," Vincent added. He loved old fashion magazines.

Alan seemed to be in shock but was actually a little preoccupied. This wasn't the time to share the news.

MONDAY

At the Kodaly Gallery's 75th-anniversary party, nearly ten years ago, Alan hoped to celebrate its 100th.

Alan had grown up at his father's gallery. He and Daphne built it beyond anything his father imagined. Suddenly, at age sixty-three, Alan was done. Frank Rizzi was taking his artists.

He was too intelligent to rail against a changing world and the change in culture. He, too, was changing.

So he and Daphne were selling. Now his family name would live on in the provenances of art they had once sold.

SOME MONTHS LATER . . .

When Taig's parents died in May, the death taxes were enormous. Taig and Daisy auctioned the art and jewelry, paid the IRS, and still had lots of money.

Taig sold the apartment building in Chelsea, retired from the NYPD, and was now working toward a doctorate in American Literature at Harvard. That meant he was in Cambridge during the week, returning home on Friday evenings.

THURSDAY

Melanie called. She was now a curator at the Rizzi Gallery in SoHo.

"Do you remember Patti Lelong?" she asked Daisy. "She was a receptionist at the Kodaly? She'd like your number. She manages a museum bookshop in Connecticut, somewhere near you."

"Wow."

Daisy wondered if she would like to see Patti. Except for tradesmen and people in shops and restaurants, she still knew very few people in Westchester County. Not that she made much effort. The local newspaper called requesting an interview and Daisy told them, "I'd rather die."

"What does she want?"

"Her boyfriend gave her a ring. Since then, she's had all kinds of trouble."

"Get rid of the ring."

"What?"

"Fun," thought Daisy. Putting on her jacket as protection against the fall wind, she went outside.

Under a willow by a clear water stream with arrowhead plants, she could see the hollow Haniwa-style heads that marked the graves for Henry Sr. and Harrietta's ashes.

"Where did the boyfriend get it?"

"At the thrift shop in Horsefly."

"Oh-ho! Someone doesn't want her to have it!"

"What do you mean?"

"I didn't see the treasures of Tutankhamun."

"Why?"

"I believe in his curse!"

"I'll let you tell Patti and vice versa, if it's all right to give her your number."

Daisy was listed in her new residence under a new name, Daisy Taig.

DAISY LAY down with a Danielle Steel and a bag of Swedish Fish, and the phone rang.

"Ms. Summerfield?"

"Yes!"

"This is Patti Lelong."

"Hi, Patti!"

"Melanie Lefkowitz gave me your number."

"Tell me about the ring! Did you have it sized—made smaller or larger?"

"No."

"Melanie said bad things happened to you since you got it. What kind of things?"

"I fell down the stairs in the house I'm living in. I rent the top floor. When I was leaving the emergency room, one of my crutches slipped and I broke my wrist."

"You were shaky!"

"It felt like someone kicked it."

"But no one was there."

"No . . ."

"And when you fell downstairs?"

"Someone pushed me."

"And no one was there."

"Do you think I'm crazy?"

"No! So the ring is from a thrift shop in Horsefly. Describe the ring," said Daisy.

"It's gold with two aquamarines."

"Are they large?"

"No."

"Little chips?"

"They're triangles."

"How are they set?"

"Two points face in the center, and the band connects to the base at either side."

"So it looks like a bow."

"I guess."

"That's a very tense design. Why not set them next to each other, or put in a tiny square knot? The woman who owned it must have died of stress!"

"Not everything in thrift shops belonged to dead people."

"If someone pushed you and no one was there, she is dead."

"What do you think I should do?"

"Meet me for a raisin scone!" Daisy said, feeling like Bunny Six.

FRIDAY

D aisy clumped down the stairs of the Horsefly Memorial House to the thrift shop.

Yesterday, she had bought an old rhinestone pin for forty dollars, a tin streetcar for twenty dollars, and a Japanese Edo cup for five dollars.

"You're late," the manager greeted her. "We almost marked you absent."

"Do you think this is real diamond?" A man showed her a piece of costume jewelry.

It was Mr. Flea.

Daisy screamed in delighted shock.

"Have you moved to Westchester County, too?"

"No-o-o-o! Up in Putnam. It was sad about the flea market but I'm getting too old to be outdoors so much anyway. Going to have a small shop in Cold Spring. You have to come up and see."

"I will!" She knew of Cold Spring, up on the Hudson, near Storm King and West Point. She'd go with Taig some weekend.

"You know, all that china you gave me, that's why I can do this. So you get a discount, anytime. What's your name again?"

It was very good to see him, but he had to get going and Daisy wanted to shop.

Daisy had glimpsed something in a carton of consignments.

Today it was in the showcase. It was an incense burner with a dog on top.

An elderly volunteer opened the case, took it out, and read the label.

"It's eighteen dollars. I don't know why they charge so much."

It had flat S handles and a brownish-gray patina with green-and-black spots.

"I'll take it."

She paid for the ancient Chinese bronze, refused to let them wrap it, put it in her car, and drove to meet Patti.

EVERY VILLAGE should have a Baker's Cafe. It was the hub of Horsefly. Right on Main Street, next to the train station, everyone in town went there.

It was prestigious to have someone from the kitchen sit at your table. Cheryl brought Daisy two small brown rectangles on a tiny plate. When Cheryl sat down, Daisy felt like the queen of Horsefly.

Cheryl said she had been baking tofu, left it in the oven too long, and invented a new snack.

Daisy loved crispy things. She wolfed them down.

"I can tell you how to make them," Cheryl said.

"No thanks."

Cheryl took the empty dish back to the kitchen as Patti Lelong arrived.

Daisy called Cheryl back over.

"We need your help. You know everything," Daisy said. "Have you seen this ring before? Show her, Patti."

Cheryl looked at it a moment and then gasped. "Oh my God! Yes, that belonged to Yolande! We all loved her."

AFTER LUNCH, Daisy drove home and examined the incense burner with her loupe.

Tiny bits of gold were caught in some of the rough patches.

She visited with the people in her tin streetcar (Municipal Railway car 504) and moved on to her lead figures. She'd been seeking them out lately, many were Tootsie Toy, Dinky, Johillco, and Britains.

Larry, a sailor, was married to Betty, a slim blond who had "notions" in her basket.

When stateside, Larry made Betty's clothes.

Joe, an enlisted man, a six-footer, had a barrel chest and a hearty laugh, "Ho, ho, ho."

Veronica, wearing a safari hat, and jodhpurs, only had one eye.

A red-bearded painter lay on a miniature fainting couch holding his palette and acting out a scene from *The Masterpiece* by Zola:

> In spite of his weariness, Claude could not keep his eyes closed, and he soon found himself wide awake, staring up at the window.

DAISY BEGAN crafting scenes.

She put a Buddha charm in a hermit's hut; a jointed blown-glass doll danced from a wire in a theater; a clay skeleton was placed in a cave.

A plastic skeleton, missing an arm and a leg, hung in a haunted room. Snippets of Harrietta's clothes were strung on wire across the opening.

She destroyed one of her own shirts and made chambray curtains for caves of waxed sandstone.

In holy arks, stones in velvet cases contained the story of creation.

"I need a camera," Daisy thought.

She glanced at her Cinderella watch, saw she was late, and hurried to the train station to pick up Taig.

SATURDAY

"I found out where she's buried!" Patti said on the phone.

"Great! So leave the ring there. It will comfort her. And when her family visits, somebody will find it. Maybe the ghost will lead one of them in the right direction," Daisy said.

Then Daphne called. "Would you like company Monday?" she asked.

MONDAY

Daisy awoke slowly in Harrietta's Duxiana, remembering her dream.

A woman with long gray hair said, "Wish I thing grap la mamba." Or was it "n-mumba?"

Taig had left without waking her.

The woman was disintegrating, but her spirit was alive. Maybe she'd return and try to talk again.

Daisy had a good reputation in the spirit world.

That was where her art came from. It didn't come from her head, and she didn't copy nature.

The self she expressed came from her work, not the other way around.

She wished she could see Harrietta, but her mother-in-law must have been absorbed in heaven's light, making it brighter.

DAISY PARKED in front of the Baker's Cafe, got a coffee, and went down to the train platform.

As she waits, we have time to observe that in the bright, hot kiln of life our characters harden as the years evaporate, covering us with a glaze of memories.

She saw the light on the engine and threw her cup in the trash.

The train came in. The doors opened. Daphne's car was far down the track.

"You look so cute!" Daisy cried, walking toward her.

"I dressed like you."

At the café, they got a table and sat down.

Daisy was so proud to be with Daphne, she wanted to stand on her chair and say, "This is who I am."

AS THEY walked around the property, Daphne asked, "Is that where Henry and Harrietta are buried? That's where I want to be, with Alan and you."

"I have to find some more heads!"

They walked into the bamboo. Joe De Leo's sculpture was gleaming.

"I'm thinking of building a photography studio," Daisy said. "Or maybe I'll build a tea room."

DAISY WAS exhausted. She would be sixty-one next month. Most afternoons, she fell asleep wearing her glasses.

"Would you like an espresso?"

"Do you know how to use that?" Daphne watched with mounting concern as Daisy tried to insert and lock the filter holder into the machine.

At last she succeeded.

In over forty years, they had never spent this much time alone together.

Daphne sat down on one of the three-legged Arne Jacobsen Ant chairs and said, "Alan is coming up. We're going to stay at the inn and look at houses tomorrow."

"Houses? What would you do out here?"

"We'll call you every morning and find out."

THE PHONE rang. It was Patti Lelong calling Daisy a genius. The ghost was no longer troubling her.

She had taken the ring to the cemetery . . .

Daisy exclaimed delightedly.

"You know what I'd like to see?" Daphne asked after Daisy finally got off the phone. "The thrift shop."

Daisy grabbed her keys.

FAVORITE BOOKS ON CHINA

Goro Akaboshi and Heiichiro Nakamaru, translated by June Silla, *Five Centuries of Korean Ceramics: Pottery and Porcelain of the Yi Dynasty*. New York: Weatherhill/Tankosha, 1975.

David Battle, General Editor, *Sotheby's Concise Encyclopedia of Porcelain*. Boston: Little, Brown, 1990.

Ada Walker Camehl, *The Blue-China Book*. New York: Dutton, 1916.

Warren E. Cox, *The Book of Pottery and Porcelain*. New York: Crown Publishers, 1944.

Lady David, *Illustrated Catalogue of Ch'ing Enameled Wares in the Percival David Foundation of Chinese Art*. London: Percival David Foundation of Chinese Art, 1958.

George Wingfield Digby, *The Work of the Modern Potter in England*. London: 1952.

Harold Donaldson Eberlein and Roger Wearne Ramsdell, *The Practical Book of Chinaware*. New York: Halcyon House, 1925.

P. J. Donnelly, *Blanc de Chine: The Porcelain of Têhua in Fukein*. New York: Praeger, 1969.

Alice Morse Earle, *China Collecting in America*. New York: Scribner's, 1892.

Eleanor J. Fox and Edward G. Fox, *Gaudy Dutch*. Pottsville, Pennsylvania, 1969.

S. Yorke Hardy, *Illustrated Catalogue of Tung, Ju, Kuan, Chün, Kuang-Tung & Glazed I-Hsing Wares in the Percival David Foundation of Chinese Art*. London: Percival David Foundation of Chinese Art, 1953.

A. L. Heatherington, *Chinese Ceramic Glazes*. London: Cambridge University Press, 1937.

W. B. Honey, *English Pottery and Porcelain*. Keeper of the Department of Ceramics Victoria and Albert Museum. London: Adam & Charles Black, 1947.

W. B. Honey, *French Porcelain of the 18th Century*. New York: Pitman, no date.

G. Bernard Hughes, *English and Scottish Earthenware 1660–1860*. New York: Macmillan, 1961.

Masahiko Kawahara, translated and adapted by Richard L. Wilson, *The Ceramic Art of Ogata Kenzan*. New York: Kodansha, 1985.

W. David Kingery and Pamela B. Vandiver, *Ceramic Masterpieces, Art, Structure, and Technology*. New York: The Free Press, 1986.

Sam Laidacker, *The American Antiques Collector, Vol. II*. Scranton, Pennsylvania, 1940–1942.

Sam Laidacker, Anglo-American China Part II, Other than American Views During the Period from 1815 to 1860. Bristol, Pennsylvania, 1951.

Sam Laidacker, *The Antique Collector, Vol. I*. Scranton, Pennsylvania, 1939–1940.

Sam Laidacker, Editor, *Standard Catalogue of Anglo-American China from 1810 to 1850*. Scranton, Pennsylvania, 1938.

Hin-Cheung Lovell, *Illustrated Catalogue of Ting Yao and Related White Wares in the Percival David Foundation of Chinese Art*. London: Percival David Foundation of Chinese Art, 1964.

Margaret Medley, *Illustrated Catalogue of Porcelains Decorated in Underglaze Blue and Copper Red in the Percival David Foundation of Chinese Art*. London: Percival David Foundation of Chinese Art, 1963.

Margaret Medley, *Illustrated Catalogue of Ming Polychrome Wares in the Percival David Foundation of Chinese Art*. London: Percival David Foundation of Chinese Art, 1966.

Maurice and Evelyn Milbourn, *Understanding Miniature British Pottery and Porcelain: 1730–Present Day*. Woodbridge, Suffolk, England: Antique Collectors Club, 1983.

Anthony Oliver, *Staffordshire Pottery: The Tribal Art of England*. London: Heinemann, 1981.

Adrian Oswald in collaboration with R. J. C. Hildyard and R. G. Hughes, *English Brown Stoneware, 1670–1900.* London: Faber & Faber, 1982.

G. Wooliscroft Rhead, *The Earthenware Collector.* New York: Dodd, Mead, 1920.

George Savage, *18th Century English Porcelain.* London: Spring Books, 1952.

Ross E. Taggart, *The Frank P. and Harriet C. Burnap Collection of English Pottery in the William Rockhill Nelson Gallery,* Revised and Enlarged Edition. Nelson Gallery–Atkins Museum, Kansas City, Missouri: 1967.

Frank Tilley, *Teapots and Tea.* Newport, England: 1957.

Richard L. Wilson, *The Art of Ogata Kenzan: Persona and Production in Japanese Ceramics.* New York: Weatherhill, 1991.

The Youngest Member, *The China Hunter's Club.* New York: Harper & Brothers: 1878.

PUBLISHER'S NOTE

M. B. Goffstein introduced her character Daisy Summerfield (as well as Paula Conrad *née* Nathanson) in 1972 in *The Underside of the Leaf.*

Some fifteen years later, Brooke discovered Manhattan's Twenty-Sixth Street flea market and knew Daisy Summerfield would love it as much as she did. Brooke wrote these stories from about 1990 to 2008 while also working on many other projects.

The town of Horsefly is based on Katonah, New York. Residents there in the 1990s will remember the Baker's Cafe that appears in *Death Goes Dutch* and *Farewell, Mr. Flea.* Cheryl is based on a real person, Brooke's friend Cheryl Weingarten.

The Blue Dragon is based on the Blue Dolphin, a longtime favorite of Brooke's, and the thrift shop in Horsefly is also based on the real one in Katonah. Brooke's memorial service was held just upstairs from the thrift shop, in the Katonah Memorial House.

•

The earlier lives of Alan and Daphne Kodaly, Daisy Summerfield, and Paula Nathanson are in *Art Girls Together: Two Novels.*

The mystery of the poems, discovered by Daisy in "The Little Notebook," is solved in *Biography of Miss Go Chi: Novelettos & Poems.*

ACKNOWLEDGMENTS

MANY THANKS to Bob and Barb Wade, Scott Sailor, Cheryl Weingarten, Kelly Raneri, Tamar Taylor, Elizabeth Denlinger, Kate Spohn, Carol Bloss and everyone at the Blue Dolphin. Very special thanks to Brooke Koven for the art and design direction and always being there.

THANKS TO EVERYONE at Girl Friday Productions, especially the splendidly skilled and smart Karen McNally Upson, for guiding this project through to its realization.

Editorial: Lisa L. Owens and Kelley Frodel
Design: Rachel Marek

CPSIA information can be obtained
at www.ICGtesting.com
Printed in the USA
LVHW041240120920
665563LV00001B/9